The Morning After . . .

Tara looked down at her hands and saw the knife she still held. She jumped and dropped it. She ran her hands over her nightgown and saw the brown stains. She looked up at Brenna with confused eyes.

"What is this?" she asked.

"Blood," Brenna said.

"Whose?"

"His?" Brenna guessed, pointing behind Tara to the body beyond.

Tara whipped her head around, saw the man in her bed, let out an ear-piercing shriek and leapt at Brenna.

"Oh, my God, who is that?"

"You don't know?" Brenna asked.

Tara shook her head.

"I'm going to see if I can rouse him," Brenna said.

She hunkered down beside the bed and, with a grunt, she gave him a shove and he flopped over.

It was the best man, and he was dead.

Berkley Prime Crime titles by Lucy Lawrence

STUCK ON MURDER
CUT TO THE CORPSE

CUT TO THE CORPSE

Lucy Lawrence

BERKLEY PRIME CRIME, NEW YORK

THE BERKLEY PUBLISHING GROUP
Published by the Penguin Group
Penguin Group (USA) Inc.
375 Hudson Street, New York, New York 10014, USA

Penguin Group (Canada), 90 Eglinton Avenue East, Suite 700, Toronto, Ontario M4P 2Y3, Canada
(a division of Pearson Penguin Canada Inc.)
Penguin Books Ltd., 80 Strand, London WC2R 0RL, England
Penguin Group Ireland, 25 St. Stephen's Green, Dublin 2, Ireland (a division of Penguin Books Ltd.)
Penguin Group (Australia), 250 Camberwell Road, Camberwell, Victoria 3124, Australia
(a division of Pearson Australia Group Pty. Ltd.)
Penguin Books India Pvt. Ltd., 11 Community Centre, Panchsheel Park, New Delhi—110 017, India
Penguin Group (NZ), 67 Apollo Drive, Rosedale, North Shore 0632, New Zealand
(a division of Pearson New Zealand Ltd.)
Penguin Books (South Africa) (Pty.) Ltd., 24 Sturdee Avenue, Rosebank, Johannesburg 2196,
South Africa

Penguin Books Ltd., Registered Offices: 80 Strand, London WC2R 0RL, England

This is a work of fiction. Names, characters, places, and incidents either are the product of the author's imagination or are used fictitiously, and any resemblance to actual persons, living or dead, business establishments, events, or locales is entirely coincidental. The publisher does not have any control over and does not assume any responsibility for author or third-party websites or their content.

CUT TO THE CORPSE

A Berkley Prime Crime Book / published by arrangement with the author

PRINTING HISTORY
Berkley Prime Crime mass-market edition / April 2010

Copyright © 2010 by Penguin Group (USA) Inc.
Excerpt from *Sealed with a Kill* by Lucy Lawrence copyright © by Penguin Group (USA) Inc.
Cover illustration by Robert Crawford.
Cover design by Rita Frangie.
Interior text design by Kristin del Rosario.

ISBN: 978-0-425-23389-4

BERKLEY® PRIME CRIME
Berkley Prime Crime Books are published by The Berkley Publishing Group,
a division of Penguin Group (USA) Inc.
375 Hudson Street, New York, New York 10014.
BERKLEY® PRIME CRIME and the PRIME CRIME logo are trademarks of Penguin Group (USA) Inc.

PRINTED IN THE UNITED STATES OF AMERICA

10 9 8 7 6 5 4 3 2 1

*For my pop, Donald McKinlay,
the best storyteller in the family.*

Acknowledgments

First and foremost, I want to give a shout out to Team Orf; Beckett, Wyatt, and the Hub. You guys keep me going every day with hugs and laughter and I love you for it.

I want to thank my agents Jacky Sach and Jessica Faust and all of the staff at BookEnds, Inc. You're the best!

Here's a nod to my wonderful editors Kate Seaver and Katherine Pelz and the fabulous PR whiz Megan Swartz and to all of the staff that I don't get to see at Berkley Prime Crime but I know are there.

I want to send hugs to the ladies of the loop and to my blog pals at Mystery Lovers' Kitchen. One of the best things about being a writer is getting to have all of you in my life.

Thanks to my extended families, the McKinlays and the Orfs. Your support means the world to me.

I also want to acknowledge the staff of the Phoenix Public Library. I have been fortunate to work there with some of the coolest people in the Valley of the Sun, and I just want to say, "You people rock!"

And lastly, I want to thank my girl Lucy. This is a dog that doesn't walk but dances, doesn't run but bounds, doesn't play but flirts. She is something special and for all the walks and hours spent patiently listening to me figure out my characters and plots, I want to say, "Thank you, sweet girl. I love you."

Chapter 1

"Did you see that?" Marie Porter hissed at her twin.

"I'd have to be stone-blind not to," Ella hissed back. "Can you believe it? Bold as brass, right in the middle of the town green, what is that boy thinking?"

"It's not what he's thinking, it's what he's thinking with," Marie said.

Brenna Miller glanced up from the display table where she was arranging a new shipment of handmade papers. Purchased from an artist in the Berkshires, these were fine papers that had been hand dyed in rich jewel tones of ruby red, sapphire blue, and emerald green. Brenna had been wondering if she could use them to decoupage a small jewelry box she had picked up at a yard sale last week, but her contemplation had been repeatedly interrupted by the elderly twins' ongoing dialogue.

The Porter sisters, Marie and Ella, were standing in front of the large bay window of Vintage Papers. They had their noses pressed to the glass and were leaning so far forward that Brenna's view of the town square was obscured by their pear-shaped backsides. Ella wore a Day-Glo yellow T-shirt with matching walking shorts and Marie wore a neon green version of the same. When she looked at them, Brenna could swear she felt her pupils dilate.

She glanced across the shop at her friend Tenley Morse, the owner of Vintage Papers. Tenley had been Brenna's best friend since their days at Boston University more than ten years ago. Tenley met Brenna's gaze with a sympathetic wink, letting Brenna know she was not alone in her exasperation with the elderly twins.

Having lived in Morse Point all their lives and with age seventy knocking on their door with a firm fist, Marie and Ella considered themselves the town's resident historians. Everyone else considered them the local blabbermouths.

"If he puts his tongue any deeper into her mouth, he's going to give her a root canal," Ella said.

"I was kissed like that once," Marie sighed. "By John Henry."

"Hunh," Ella grunted. "Too bad he thought he was kissing me."

"He did not," Marie huffed.

"He did, too," Ella returned. "You stole him and you know it."

Brenna stepped forward and wedged herself in between the two ladies, pushing her auburn head in between their curly gray ones. She was afraid they were about to come to blows over the legendary John Henry; it had happened before, and it behooved her to protect Tenley's shop from harm for job security reasons if nothing else.

Marie and Ella continued to scowl at each other around her, but Brenna didn't budge.

"Is that Jake Haywood with Tara Montgomery?" she asked. "I heard they got engaged."

Both ladies were immediately diverted.

"Last week," Marie confirmed. "I was at Totally Polished getting a manicure when I heard Margie Haywood tell Ruby Wolcott that Jake even called Tara's parents and asked permission."

"And they gave it?" Tenley asked from across the room. Her blue eyes were wide with surprise.

"Apparently, little Miss Tara gets what little Miss Tara wants," Ella said. "And now she wants Jake."

"You mean 'for now' she wants Jake," Marie said.

"Well, she'd better be sure, because if he marries that girl, it's forever," Ella said. "There has never been a divorce in the Haywood family."

"Nope, they're like swans, they mate for life," Marie agreed. Her voice sounded wistful, and Brenna had to admit that nowadays that did sound rare and romantic.

Brenna glanced out the window. Jake Haywood wore gray coveralls smeared with grease, tan leather work boots, and a red rag half hanging out of his back pocket. By contrast, Tara wore a Juicy Couture summer sundress that was buttercup yellow and sported a charming bow in the front. Her feet were encased in matching yellow ballet flats and her long blond hair was held back by a wide white headband.

Jake nuzzled her neck, but when she would have pressed herself against him, he held her back in an obvious attempt to keep her dress free from his grease stains. Tara tossed her hair over her shoulder and giggled up at him, and the young man, who Brenna had thought so serious, well, at least he had been when he fixed the brakes on her Jeep last month, grinned down at the delicate girl before him with his heart in his eyes.

Brenna sighed and then realized that Ella, Marie, and Tenley had sighed at the exact same moment.

As they watched, Tara took three steps back from Jake and then leapt into his arms, giving him no choice but to catch her. Accepting defeat in the battle to keep her dress unmarred, Jake held her close and kissed her with a thoroughness that left Brenna breathless.

She quickly looked away, feeling as if she were intruding on the young couple. She glanced at the others; judging by the flush on everyone else's cheeks, she knew she wasn't the only one affected.

"Ladies," Brenna said. They paid her no mind. "Ella! Marie!" she snapped, forcibly drawing their attention from the young couple.

"What?" Ella snapped, her reverie broken.

"It's rude to stare," Brenna said.

"Rude? I'll tell you what's rude. Jake was a perfectly well-mannered boy until *she* came around," Marie said with an indignant sniff. She sounded jealous.

"*She* being Tara?" Brenna asked. "What's wrong with Tara?"

"She's not from around here," Ella said, as if that were explanation enough.

"Neither am I," Brenna reminded them.

"That's different, dear," Marie said comfortingly. "Last April, when you solved the mayor's murder, you proved you're one of us. Besides, Tenley Morse is your friend and her family founded Morse Point."

"You can't get a better recommendation than that," Ella concurred.

Brenna glanced over her shoulder at Tenley, who was hiding her laughter behind a large book of wedding invitation samples.

"Be that as it may," Brenna said, "I don't see what's wrong with a little kissing between engaged persons. In fact, I think it's sweet."

As the three women glanced back out the window at the young couple, Nate Williams strolled by. His feet faltered when he saw the three of them pressed against the glass. His gaze met Brenna's and the corner of his mouth turned up in a small smile. She had no doubt he was amused to find her wedged between the Porter twins like a slice of olive loaf between two pieces of rye. She would have shrugged but her arms were pinned to her sides.

His silver gaze glinted as he made his way toward the door of the shop. The jangle of the string of bells on the door made the twins hop off their perch to check out the new arrival. They fairly lit up at the sight of Nate, who was known to be reclusive and seldom darkened the door of any store other than the grocery.

"Hi, Tenley, ladies," he said, acknowledging Ella and Marie. "I was wondering if I could borrow Brenna for a bit."

"Hi, Nate," Tenley answered naturally, as if it weren't at all unusual for Nate to be in her shop. "Go right ahead. Just have her back in time to teach her class."

"Will do," he said. "Brenna?"

She could feel the Porter sisters' matching inquisitive gazes boring into her back as she slid out of the window and walked toward the door where Nate waited.

"Don't tell me my rent is overdue," she joked.

"No, but I do have some landlord–tenant business to discuss with you," he said. He looked serious, and Brenna felt a flicker of doubt ignite inside of her.

Nate Williams had once been a world famous artist, who abruptly retired from the New York art scene ten years ago. He had relocated to Morse Point, Massachusetts, after his retirement, and other than being the chief suspect in a murder investigation three months ago, he had managed to live a very quiet life here. He owned several cabins on the shore of Morse Point Lake, one of which Brenna had been renting from him for a little more than a year.

"Is something wrong?" she asked as she followed him outside.

He led the way down the sidewalk, away from the big ears of the twins. Brenna matched his longer stride and waited for him to explain.

At the corner, he turned to face her. His slate gray gaze was as intense as ever, giving Brenna the impression that they were completely alone as opposed to standing on a busy street corner.

"Did you catch the game last night?" he asked.

She might have known. He wanted to talk baseball. Nate was a devout Yankee fan, while Brenna was a card-carrying member of the Red Sox Nation.

"Talk to the hand," she said and put hers up between them. She turned and resumed walking. She figured she might as well grab a latte at Stan's Diner while she was out and about.

"Oh, what's the matter?" he asked. "Is the taste of defeat a little bitter?"

"It was only the first game in the series," she said. "There are two to go, and I'm quite sure I'll be the one gloating then."

"Gloating?" he repeated. "I'm not gloating."

"Oh, please," she said, pulling the door to the diner open, "if you looked any more smug, I'd think you batted in the winning run yourself."

Nate grinned, and Brenna felt her pupils dilate again, but this time in a good way. With his perpetually tousled brown hair, sharp masculine features, and lean runner's build, Nate Williams was the best looking bachelor in town. Hands down.

Okay, maybe her friend Tenley would argue that Matt Collins, the bartender at the Fife and Drum, was the hottest single man in town, but for Brenna, it was Nate. Too bad he seemed to see her as just a friend.

She took a seat at the counter and Nate sat beside her.

She was surprised. Nate didn't come into town often and when he did, he didn't linger.

"So why were you and the Porter twins plastered to the window?" he asked.

"Jake Haywood and Tara Montgomery," she explained.

Nate looked bewildered, so she spun on her stool and pointed through the window to the young couple now walking hand in hand across the town square.

"And they would be of interest because . . . ?"

"She's not from around here," Brenna explained. She was glad to see that Nate looked as confused as she had once been.

"Can I take your order?" Marybeth DeFalco asked from behind the counter.

"A latte, please," Brenna said. "Heavy on the froth."

"I'll have the same but little to no froth," Nate said.

"But that's the best part," Brenna said.

"Not if you're a man," he said. "Men don't do froth."

"Fine, can I have his then?" Brenna asked.

Marybeth studied them for a moment. She had been giving the Porter twins a run for the money in the gossip race, mostly because she was married to Officer DeFalco, a local cop, and was therefore privy to inside information. Brenna knew Marybeth was sizing up the situation and trying to choose the best way to determine what Brenna and Nate were doing together. She decided to cut Marybeth off at the knees.

"Separate checks, please," Brenna said with a small smile. Marybeth nodded with understanding.

Nate gave her a look.

"What?" she asked. "Did you want to be served up as the latest dish?"

"Huh?" he asked.

"You really need to get out more," she said. "If you

buy me a cup of coffee, the whole town will be speculating as to whether we're dating."

"And why do we care what other people think?" Nate propped his chin on his hand as he studied her. She could tell by the crinkles in the corners of his eyes that he found this conversation amusing.

"Let's just say that I don't want to be in Tara Montgomery's shoes," Brenna said.

"Why? What's wrong with her shoes?" he asked. "Broken heel?"

Brenna grinned. He was teasing her by being deliberately obtuse, and it was charming. Still, just because Nate didn't care what anyone thought of him, didn't mean Brenna was about to let herself become an overmined vein of gossip for Morse Point.

She'd had more than her share of attention when she'd first arrived in town. She was just beginning to feel accepted, and she wasn't about to blow it by drawing attention to herself.

"Tara is from Boston," she explained. "She's marrying a local man, and the residents are still undecided if this is a good thing or not."

· Nate spun on his chair to look out the window. Tara and Jake were still holding hands as they walked down the sidewalk toward the garage where Jake worked.

Haywood Auto, owned and operated by Jake's father for the past thirty years, was where everyone in town took their cars. Everyone had a John Haywood story.

Lillian Page, the town librarian and mother of five boys ages two to twelve, had recently raced into Haywood Auto, convinced her minivan was about to blow up because it was making scary knocking noises. Turned out it was marbles in the gas tank. John got the marbles out and only charged her ten dollars because he said it was worth the laugh as she chased the boys around the garage, threatening to send them to their rooms for so long they'd think they were mattresses.

John Haywood was everyone's favorite mechanic, and his son Jake was following in his father's footsteps. Or at least he was, until he fell in love with Tara Montgomery.

"I don't see how it's anyone's business," Nate said. "If they're happy, people should just butt out."

"Damn straight," a gruff voice said from behind them.

Brenna spun around to see Stan, the owner and cook of Stan's Diner, standing behind them with their lattes. Stan was a beefy, red-faced man, who had retired from the U.S. Navy twenty plus years ago and still looked as if he'd be more comfortable with a rolling deck under his feet instead of solid linoleum flooring. He was an artist in the kitchen, however, and today he had shaped the froth on Brenna's latte into a five-petal flower sprinkled with nutmeg.

"Thanks, Stan," she said. He nodded and she realized that the two words he'd just uttered were the most conversation she'd ever gotten out of him.

Stan lumbered away, and Brenna turned back to Nate. "So, tell me, what really brought you into town?"

"You, actually," he said.

Chapter 2

Brenna felt the hot coffee warm her hand through the thick ceramic mug almost to the point of discomfort, and yet, she didn't let go. Some months before, she had realized that she had a very unwelcome crush on Nate Williams. Mostly it was unwelcome because she didn't think he regarded her as anything more than a tenant/friend.

Still, it was physically impossible to ignore the warm flush of hope that filled her at his words. She took a bracing sip of coffee, hoping she had not just given herself a frothy mustache while she waited for him to continue.

"I need to go out of town for a few days," he said, "and I was wondering if you would mind babysitting Hank?"

Hank was Nate's exuberant golden retriever. Brenna had a crush on him almost as big as the one she had on Nate.

"I'd love to," she said, and meant it. If she was disappointed at not being asked out by Nate, which she had known was pretty much out of the realm of possibility, she was buoyed by getting to have Hank for a few days.

"Thanks," he said. "He worships you, and I'd worry about him if I left him with anyone else."

"When do you leave?" she asked. She knew that asking where, which was what she really wanted to know, would be too intrusive, so she hoped this was a nice roundabout way of digging for information.

"Tomorrow," he said.

Okay, so much for the roundabout route.

"I'll be back on Monday," he said.

Brenna nodded. Her one bedroom cabin sat across a small inlet from Nate's. She often sat on her porch in the evening, especially now that the June nights were warm, and watched the sun set across the water. Because Nate seldom went out, his lights were usually on. She realized it was going to be odd to look across the lake and see his cabin dark. At least she'd have Hank for company.

"Thanks, Brenna," he said. "I owe you one."

"No problem," she said. She glanced at her watch. "Is that the time? Ack, I have to go. I have to teach a class."

She hopped off her stool and fished the money out of her pocket for the coffee, but Nate closed his hand over hers.

"No," he said. "It's on me."

Brenna could feel Marybeth watching them from down the counter. Nate followed her glance and shook his head at her.

"I don't care what anyone says," he said. His silver gaze was intent upon hers. "It's on me."

"You're just asking for trouble," she said but knew there would be no talking him out of it. "Thanks for the coffee. I'll be home late tonight. Can you bring Hank over before you leave tomorrow?"

"Sure," he said. "And thanks again."

"My pleasure," she said as she hurried toward the door. She refused to wonder about where he was going and why.

Really, it was none of her business. And maybe if she told herself that twenty times, she'd believe it. *Yeah, right.*

Brenna hurried back up the street to Vintage Papers. She had a decoupage class to prep for and she was looking forward to tonight's project.

The bells jangled on the door as she entered, and Tenley glanced up at her from the worktable in the back.

The table was covered in blue vinyl, and she had already begun to put out the scissors and glue for tonight's class.

"Did he ask you out?" Tenley asked, looking hopeful.

"No," Brenna said. She tried to keep the disappointment out of her voice, but Tenley gave her a sympathetic look anyway.

"What did he want then?"

"I'm babysitting Hank for a few days," Brenna said.

"Oh? Where's he going?" Tenley asked. She fussed with a box of cutouts, trying to make them look neat.

"I don't know," Brenna said. "I didn't ask."

Tenley frowned at her. "You're watching his dog. You're allowed to ask."

"It felt nosey," Brenna said. "If he wanted me to know, he would have told me."

"If you say so," Tenley said. "The Porter twins are going to tell everyone that you're dating, you know."

"That's okay," she said. "He insisted on buying me coffee, so Marybeth DeFalco will probably start telling everyone that I'm expecting his child."

Tenley laughed out loud, and Brenna shrugged. "I tried to warn him."

Brenna stored most of her decoupage projects in a large armoire at the back of the shop. On the upper shelves, there were small letter boxes, breakfast trays, a wooden canister set, and a few other small items, all placed strategically for sale by Tenley.

The armoire itself was one of Brenna's prized pieces. Not that she wouldn't sell it if the price was right, but she had spent an entire summer working on it and was quite attached to it. Rescued from a secondhand shop in Boston, she had painted it a rich blood red and then used old images of powder-wigged lords and their delicate-waisted ladies to decorate each of the bottom three drawers and the cupboard doors above. It had a decided Louis XIV flavor to it, and though it matched nothing, Brenna loved it. Tenley loved it, too, and had badgered Brenna until she agreed to let her use it in the shop.

Brenna stashed many of her rare papers in the bottom drawers of the armoire as well as supplies that she gathered for her classes. It was the bottom drawer she opened now as she hefted out a stack of clear glass plates she had purchased at a party rental place that was going out of business. The plates were square in shape with a narrow lip around the edges.

She had checked each plate to make sure it was free of chips or bubbles. These were in mint condition and tonight she was going to use them to teach her students to do decoupage under glass.

She put a plate in front of each chair and then took two plate holders out of the bottom drawer of the armoire. In the second drawer she had two plates that she had already decoupaged and she put them on display one, in each plate holder at the end of each table.

One she had decorated with cutouts of antique keys and then backed with several thick coats of creamy white latex paint. She used this plate as a key holder. The other she had covered in cutouts of old coins from all over the world. When she looked at the top of the clear glass plate, the copper, silver, and gold coins adhered faceup on the bottom of the plate and then painted over in forest green paint made it appear almost as if real coins were scattered across the dish. She ran her fingers across the smooth glass surface, pleased with how well the plate had turned out.

"Those look fantastic," Tenley said.

"Let's hope the class thinks so," Brenna said.

The bells jangled on the front door and the first few students trickled in. The Porter sisters were first, followed by Lillian Page the local librarian and Sarah Buttercomb, who owned the bakery on the corner. Sarah was carrying a pink box full of sugar cookies. She frequently brought leftovers from the bakery, much to the delight of the class.

Margie Haywood came in a few minutes later. She was married to John Haywood and had been the school nurse at Morse Point Elementary for forever and a day. There wasn't a knee under the age of twenty that she hadn't stuck a Band-Aid on.

Margie was one of the cornerstones of Morse Point, and as president of the women's auxiliary, she ran their annual June rummage sale, which raised funds for the community. She was short and gently rounded with close-cropped dark brown hair that was slowly fading to gray. She doled out hugs as easily as others gave hellos, and she was one of Brenna's favorite students.

With Margie came Tara Montgomery and another woman, who looked to be a slightly older version of Tara. Her features were delicate like Tara's but had a maturity about them that no amount of cosmetic surgery could erase. She wore her blond hair in a neat blunt cut that ended at her shoulders. Unlike Margie, this woman was not rounded with middle age but rail thin. Her clothes were cut perfectly to fit her narrow frame, and it was easy to see that there were no sales racks in her life. Brenna knew right away she must be Tara's mother.

The Porter sisters exchanged a look with raised eyebrows, but wisely said nothing. Margie brought Tara and her mother over to Brenna.

"Brenna, I hope you don't mind, but I thought I'd bring Tara and Tiffany to class tonight to meet some of my friends," Margie said.

"Not at all," Brenna said and she shook Tara's out-stretched hand and then Tiffany's. Both women gave her a solid, warm handshake. There were no cold, limp-wristed women here.

Tara was even prettier close up, with large sky blue eyes and a cute upturned nose. Brenna could see why Jake Haywood had fallen for her.

"Tara is marrying my son Jake," Margie said. Her eyes were wide when she said it. The engagement was only a week old, so Brenna figured she must still be trying to wrap her brain around gaining a daughter-in-law.

"Congratulations," Tenley said as she joined them. "And welcome to Morse Point."

"Thank you," Tara said with a smile so genuine it was infectious. "It's such a lovely town. I just know Jake and I are going to be so happy here."

"Margie, you're going to have to draft this young lady to help with the rummage sale," Lillian said. "We're try-ing to raise funds for new police cars."

"Really?" Tara asked. "I'd love to help."

"Then start going through your closet for donations," Sarah said. "It's an excellent excuse to refresh your ward-robe."

The ladies all laughed.

"That reminds me, Margie, I have a couple of items in the back," Brenna said. "Can you take a look and tell me if they're what you're looking for?"

"Sure," Margie said and followed Brenna into the work-room.

Brenna had several designer suits she'd worn in her former life, working in an art gallery in Boston, hanging in the break room. She'd brought them in knowing she was going to see Margie. It felt like a bold maneuver to donate them to the rummage sale. As if she were making an official break from her old life and embracing this new one.

"These are exquisite," Margie said. She ran her hand over a plastic-covered, plum Nicole Miller. "Several steps up from what I'm donating at any rate."

Margie gestured down at her feet and Brenna saw she was wearing a pair of tan work boots.

"You really want to part with those?" Brenna asked. "They could be pretty spiffy with some hot pink laces."

Margie smiled but it was rimmed with sadness. "They're Jake's. He outgrew them before he even scuffed them. I've been using them in the garden, but they're too good to keep for myself. It seems like just yesterday he and Clue were catching tadpoles in the lake and begging to keep them as pets, and now he's getting married."

"Lillian says once you're a parent the days are long and the years short," Brenna said. She looped her arm around Margie's shoulders and led her back out into the main room. "It'll be all right."

"Maybe you could donate some of your furs, Mom," Tara was saying as they rejoined them.

Tiffany gave Tara a weak smile, and Brenna knew she was clearly not as enamored of the thought of her furs in the rummage sale as her daughter.

Brenna glanced over at the Porter sisters. They both looked disapproving and she hoped they didn't give Tara or her mother a hard time.

"Why don't you ladies help yourself to some wine and cheese?" Brenna said, and she led the way to the refreshment table. On the way, she leaned close to the Porter sisters and hissed, "Be nice."

They both gave her wide-eyed innocent looks, and she shook her head. This was going to be a long class.

Tenley brought two chairs from the break room and shifted the places at the table to make room for the Montgomery women, while Brenna grabbed two more clear glass plates from the armoire. Tara oohed and aahed over Brenna's work and even her mother seemed impressed.

When all of the women were seated, Brenna had them sift through the baskets of paper cutouts until they found enough to use on their plates. She then had them turn their plates upside down and glue the pictures facedown onto the glass.

"That's a lovely engagement ring, Tara," Lillian said as she leaned over to grab a bottle of white glue. "It's very delicate."

"Thank you," Tara said. She turned her hand in the light to watch the diamond sparkle. "It was Jake's grandmother's."

Margie gave her a wistful smile. "My mother wore that ring from the day Daddy proposed until the day she died."

"And I will, too," Tara said. She clutched her hand to her chest, looking painfully earnest.

Brenna glanced at the ring. A small round diamond was nestled in the center of an ornate gold filigree ring. It looked very Art Deco, which would be about the right time for Jake's grandmother to have been engaged.

The diamond was not the usual size that someone of Tara's social standing would normally wear. Brenna glanced at Tiffany's hand and noticed she wore several diamond rings, all of which dwarfed the petite diamond on Tara's hand.

Tiffany took Tara's hand in hers to study the ring. "It has an old-fashioned charm," she said. "It's a lovely starter ring."

Margie bit her lip, and Brenna couldn't tell if she was holding back a sharp retort or if it was a reaction to having her feelings hurt.

"Does everyone have their pictures glued on?" Brenna asked, swiftly changing the subject.

Ella Porter was just gluing on her last picture. She wiped the excess glue off of the glass with a damp rag and looked up at the rest of the table.

"Okay, we're going to let these dry until our next class, and when we come back, we're going to paint the back of the plate with latex paint. I have several colors here, but you're welcome to bring your own. When the paint is dry, we will then seal it with polyacrylic to protect it from chipping. So start thinking about what color you want to use for your backing."

"I'm so glad I get to come back," Tara said. She had chosen several ornate spoon cutouts, and Brenna noted that she had done a nice job with her layout. "Aren't you, Mother?"

Tiffany glanced at the plain plate in front of her. She had done nothing with it. "I don't think that will be necessary."

A low buzz of conversation began amongst the students, while Brenna and Tenley began cleaning up after the night's class.

Brenna was carrying a tray full of white glue bottles into the break room when Tiffany Montgomery approached her.

"I was wondering if I could speak to you, Brenna?" she asked.

"Sure." She motioned for Tiffany to follow her into the break room, where they also stored their supplies, while she checked the tops on the glue bottles and put them back on their shelf.

"I had an inspiration during your class," she said. "I've been trying to think of a clever wedding favor, Jordan almonds are just so last century, and while I was sitting in your class, it hit me."

Brenna wiped a spot of glue off of the tray and turned to give Tiffany her full attention.

"I want to hire you to decoupage something brilliant for Tara's wedding favors," she said.

"Okay," Brenna said slowly, not wanting to appear unreceptive. "What did you have in mind?"

"Well, we're inviting three hundred people, and I'm sure they'll all come, so it has to be something that you can do in the next two months."

"Three hundred wedding favors?" Brenna asked. "Wow."

"I know it's a lot, but just think what a boost it will be for the shop and for your personal business," Tiffany said.

"I'll have to talk to Tenley and see if she can help," Brenna said.

"Absolutely," Tiffany said. "I'm willing to pay top dollar for your time. Since this is Tara's first wedding, I want to go all out."

"First wedding?" Brenna asked.

"Certainly," Tiffany lowered her voice. "You don't really think she'll stay married to a mechanic, do you? We raised her to have higher expectations than that."

"But she loves him," Brenna said. "In fact, I don't think I've ever seen two people more in love."

Tiffany sighed. "Yes, she loves him today and probably for a year or two, but then, she's going to want to have children, and she won't want to raise them here in this limited suburbia. She'll want to raise them in Boston where they can have every advantage. Don't get me wrong, I like Jake. He seems like a fine young man, but I don't see him leaving Morse Point, and I don't see Tara staying."

"So, why throw such an elaborate wedding?" Brenna asked. "If you think it's doomed to fail, why not encourage them to live together?"

"Because a big wedding is what Tara wants," she said, as if it were obvious.

Brenna felt an ominous thumping behind her eye. She had been born and raised in Boston by parents not much different than Tara's. Their life was a whirlwind of society events and exotic travel. They could no more see what a town like Morse Point had to offer than they could understand why some people preferred it.

In their high society world, your value was equal to the sum of your bank statement and the worth of your personal possessions. In Morse Point, your value was based upon what you contributed to the local community and the sort of person that you were, hardworking or lazy, kind or cruel.

Brenna knew she preferred to be judged by the latter and she also knew that her parents didn't understand it, which was undoubtedly why they had yet to come and see her here.

"I'll see what I can come up with," she said and was surprised when Tiffany gave her a gentle squeeze and an air-kiss.

"Fabulous, I'll pop in tomorrow and we can brainstorm some ideas," Tiffany said.

"Oh, okay," Brenna said, feeling as if she'd just been tied to the train tracks.

"You're a dear, Brenna," she said. "When I heard that Justin and Joan Miller's daughter was living out in the wild, I thought I'd find you wearing a lot of plaid flannel and letting yourself go, but you look quite lovely."

"You know my parents then?" Brenna asked faintly.

"Just in passing," Tiffany said. "We've shared a box at the opera once or twice."

"Oh," Brenna said.

"I'm sure your mother will be happy to hear how well you look next time I see her."

"Thank you," Brenna said. She swallowed the urge to beg Tiffany not to mention seeing her to her parents. But that would be awkward at best; still, it was a tough impulse to ignore.

Tiffany left the break room with a wave of her hand, and Brenna glanced at her reflection in the small mirror on the back of the door. Thank the fashion gods that it was June, and it was too warm for her to wear her favorite flannel shirt. Instead, she was in a snug pair of Mudd jeans and a black eyelet tank top from Talbots. Her shoulder length, curly auburn hair was twisted into a knot on the top of her head, from which a few curly strands had escaped, softening the severity of the hairdo and framing her green brown eyes becomingly.

"Good news!" Tenley stuck her head around the door.

"What's that?" Brenna asked, looking away from the mirror and focusing on her friend.

"They're all gone!" Tenley announced, and Brenna laughed.

They walked back into the empty shop together and while they finished cleaning, Brenna told Tenley about her conversation with Tiffany.

"Awfully pessimistic, isn't she?" Tenley asked. "I wondered when I heard the Montgomerys gave Jake their permission. Now it all makes sense. They don't expect it to last."

"And how about those wedding favors?" Brenna asked. "Three hundred of them for a doomed marriage. I have no idea what to do about that."

"You'll come up with something," Tenley assured her. "You're brilliant, and it will be a fantastic showcase for your work and the shop."

"Promise you'll help?" Brenna asked.

"Absolutely," she said.

A soft rap on the glass front door interrupted their conversation. Outside stood Tara.

Tenley crossed the room to open the door.

"Hi, Tara," she said. "What brings you back? Did you forget something?"

"No," she said. "Mother just told me that Brenna has agreed to make my wedding favors, and I just wanted to come back and say thank you. I think they will just be so wonderful."

"You're welcome," Brenna said. She was uncomfortable with Tara's gushing exuberance. It curled her tongue like too much sugar in a glass of iced tea, but Tara seemed so sincere, Brenna forced a smile through her discomfort. "It's my pleasure."

"I'll see you tomorrow then," Tara said. With a wave and a twirl of her skirt, she whirled back out the door.

Tenley closed and locked it behind her.

"Is she for real?" she asked.

"I think so," Brenna said. "I don't get *fake* coming off of her."

"Me neither," Tenley said. "She's just so perky and bubbly. It's unnatural. That girl really needs an off switch."

"She's ten years younger than us," Brenna observed. "Maybe at thirty-two, our on-off is more intermittent, like windshield wipers."

"You think?" A worry line creased Tenley's forehead and she reached for the wine bottle on the refreshment table. It was empty. She made a sad face.

"Let's go to the Fife and Drum and have a glass of wine," Brenna suggested.

"Best idea I've heard all day." Tenley smiled and went to retrieve their purses.

Brenna watched her go and wondered if the sudden spring in her step had more to do with seeing Matt Collins, the bartender at the Fife and Drum, than it did a glass of wine. She couldn't help but notice that Tenley was showing shades of Tara's peppiness. She wasn't foolish enough to point it out, however.

* * *

The sun was just kissing the horizon awake when a gentle knock sounded at Brenna's door, followed by a frenzy of barking. Brenna padded across the hardwood floor of her cabin, wishing she had taken the time to at least comb her hair when she got up.

Not that it mattered. As soon as the door opened a crack, Hank launched himself at her and began to lick her face. No one was ever as happy to see her as Hank.

She gently pushed him off and he ran into the house. He lapped the main room three times, kicking up area rugs as his nails scratched against the floor. He bounded into the bedroom, and Brenna heard the springs on her queen-sized bed give a groan when Hank landed on it with a thud.

She could see him through the doorway, feet in the air and head on her pillow, looking as happy as a dog could be without a juicy bone in his mouth.

"I can see he's going to suffer real separation anxiety while I'm gone," Nate said.

Brenna turned to see him enter the cabin, lugging a leash, two bowls, and a bag of food.

"I'll show him your picture every day," she offered.

Nate grinned. "He'll probably think you're trying to punish him. My cell phone number is taped to his bag of food if you need to reach me."

"Any special instructions?" she asked.

"I'd say don't spoil him, but what would be the point?" he asked.

"Indeed," she agreed.

"Seriously, thank you," Nate said. "It helps knowing he's in good hands."

An awkward silence fell between them while they watched Hank wrestle with Brenna's pale blue cotton sheets. He looked as if he were burrowing into the bed for a long doze.

"Lucky dog," Nate said.

Brenna turned to find his steady gray gaze regarding her. There were so many things she wanted to ask him, like where was he going and why? But caution held her silent. Nate was deeply private and she felt as if he'd let her into his world more than most. She didn't want to get the boot by being too inquisitive.

So she smiled and said, "Call anytime you want a Hank update. I'll either be here or at the shop and I always have my cell phone on me."

"I will," he said. "Bye, Hank, be good."

Hank barked and wiggled farther down into the bed.

Brenna followed Nate to the door, and when he opened it, a sliver of warm June air brushed by her.

He stepped onto the porch and turned back to face her. Again, Brenna felt awkward. They were friends, but not like she and Tenley were friends. If Tenley left town for a few days, Brenna would hug her. She had no idea what to do with Nate, so she settled for a small wave.

He lifted his hand to wave back. He opened his mouth as if he was going to say something more but then shook his head. Shoving his hands into his pockets, he turned on his heel and walked down the three front porch steps onto the grass beyond. Brenna closed the door and moved to the window to watch him walk toward the communal parking lot they all shared. It was cold comfort to think that he didn't know what to do with her either.

As soon as she stepped away from the window, Hank bounded out of her bed. He paced back and forth in front of the door, leaving her with no doubt as to what he wanted.

"Okay, okay, I'll take you for a W-A-L-K," she said. She spelled the word, knowing from previous experience that Hank would go mental if she said it out loud. Judging by the way his ears pricked up and his tail wagged, however, she feared he was becoming quite the speller.

"Just a quick one," she said as she went to get dressed. "I have to meet Tara and her mother in the shop this morning, and I still haven't got any ideas for the wedding favors."

Hank barked. Brenna appreciated his vote of confidence. Too bad she didn't believe him.

Chapter 3

Brenna was twenty minutes late. Normally, this would not be a problem, but when she pulled into an empty spot in front of Vintage Papers and saw the silver Lexus next to her, her heart sank. She hoped the Montgomerys hadn't been waiting long.

She hit the lock button on her key fob and the Jeep gave a honk of confirmation that all the doors were locked. Despite having lived in Morse Point for over a year and a half now, Brenna was still vigilant about locking her car and house. She knew most of the townsfolk thought she was crazy, but after the town mayor was murdered a few months ago, Brenna saw no reason to be lax. Having grown up in Boston, locking doors and carrying pepper spray came as naturally to her as breathing.

She pulled open the door to the shop, and sure enough, Tiffany and Tara were sitting at the worktable in the back of the room, looking through several paper sample books while Tenley served them hot tea and sugar cookies.

"I am so sorry to keep you waiting," Brenna apologized. "I'm dog sitting and, well, he has a mind of his own and a short walk turned into a long jog."

"Don't think on it," Tiffany assured her. "We've been looking at some of your pieces. You are quite talented."

"Thank you," Brenna said. "That's very kind of you to say."

She sat in the chair opposite the two women and Tenley sat beside her, pushing a delicate Haviland china cup in her direction.

Brenna absently added a dollop of honey to the steaming tea and admired the pretty yellow roses that decorated the side of the cup. That's when inspiration struck.

"What sort of flowers are you having for your bouquet?" she asked Tara.

"Oh, we found the most wonderful florist," she enthused. "I'm going to carry yellow and red roses mixed with red pyracantha berries and surrounded by yellow calla lilies. It's breathtaking."

Brenna smiled. This might work. She especially liked the berries part.

"What do you think of using a glass votive with a scented candle in it for your wedding favor?"

Tara's eyes lit up while Tiffany looked thoughtful. Brenna glanced at Tenley. Tara could like it all she wanted but it was Tiffany who would make the final decision as this was really her show.

"Tell me more," Tiffany said.

"I'll do better than that," Brenna said. "Let me see if I can show you what I mean."

She went over to the armoire and began to search through the drawers. In the bottom she found a plain glass votive. She fished through her box of specialty papers until she came up with a stem covered in red berries and a yellow rose.

"We could decoupage flowers and berries to the glass," she said. "Then we could put a layer of tissue paper over it to give it a frosted look."

Tiffany sat up straighter. Brenna could tell she liked what she was hearing.

"I like it," Tiffany said. "But it doesn't really commemorate the day."

"Think of all the wedding favors you've gotten with a couple's name and date on them. Unless they're edible, they just become one more thing stuffed in a closet somewhere. This would be something people could use again," Brenna said.

"She's right, Mother," Tara said. "I have boxes of wedding favors with no place to go."

"You know, we could get monogrammed candles to put into the votives," Tenley said. "I bet we could go to a candlemaker and have them create a specially scented candle with your initials on it and then we could put them in Brenna's votives."

"I love it," Tiffany declared. Tara beamed.

"Excellent," Brenna said. She could have kissed Tenley for coming up with the monogrammed candle idea. "I'll make up a few in different colors and sizes and then you can tell me what you prefer."

"In the meantime, I'll start calling local candlemakers," Tiffany said. "I'm not going to tell Sheri, our wedding planner, because I don't want her to steal the idea for one of her other clients. We'll just tell her it's under control."

She rose from the table, looking satisfied. Brenna tried not to sag with relief.

"Tara, we need to go. We have another fitting for your gown," Tiffany said.

"Yes, Mother," Tara said. As she passed Brenna, she leaned down and gave her a fierce hug. "Thank you so much."

"You're welcome," Brenna said and squeezed her back. She was getting used to Tara's exuberance; in fact, to her surprise, she was becoming fond of it.

Tara then turned and gave Tenley a hug, too.

"I think we three are just going to be the best of friends," Tara said. "Oh, that gives me an idea!"

"What's that?" Brenna asked.

"I think you two should really come out with me and my bridesmaids tonight," Tara said.

Tenley and Brenna exchanged a look. Bachelorette parties were right up there with standing in line at the DMV and annual gynecological exams for Brenna, and she was pretty sure Tenley felt the same way.

"Oh, I'm dog sitting . . ." Brenna began.

"Oh, please," Tara begged. "My maid of honor, Britney, just flew in from Paris and she won't be back until the wedding. Please say you'll join us."

Tiffany reappeared behind her daughter.

"Join who?" she asked.

"Tara just invited us to her bachelorette party," Tenley said. "And we'd like to, but . . ."

"But what?" Tiffany interrupted. One perfectly waxed eyebrow lifted slightly higher than the other while she waited for their answer.

"But, of course, we'd love to," Tenley said.

Brenna gaped at her as if she'd recently sustained a head injury.

"Excellent," Tiffany said and turned back to the door.

"Yay!" Tara said with a small jump and a clap. "We'll meet in the bar at the Fife and Drum at eight o'clock."

"See you then," Tenley said with a wave.

"Are you kidding me? Why did you say yes?" Brenna asked as soon as the door shut behind them. "I hate those things."

"I'm sorry," Tenley said. "But Tiffany reminded me so

much of my mother, I cracked under the eyebrow of displeasure."

"It is a powerful eyebrow," Brenna acknowledged. "But still, that's no excuse. You and I are veterans in the 'making your mother unhappy' wars. We need to get out of this."

"Think of it as a deed for the greater good," Tenley reasoned.

"How do you figure?"

"Being seen with us will give Tara some credibility in the town," Tenley explained. "You heard how the Porter sisters talked about her. Someone needs to show acceptance of this union if Tara is going to stand a chance of getting her happy ever after."

"That would be you," Brenna said. "You're Morse Point's favorite native daughter. I'm still a stranger in these parts."

"Not anymore you're not," Tenley said. "Come on, it'll be fun."

"Fun? Do you remember Donna Smithfield's bachelorette party?"

Tenley cringed, but Brenna was merciless.

"Her maid of honor paraded her all over Boston, wearing a veil with tiny penises all over it. It was bizarre and weird. Not to mention I had a hangover for three days."

Tenley burst out laughing. "That was seven years ago. Get over it already."

"I'm not wearing anything with man junk on it," Brenna said.

"I think you're safe," Tenley said. "As far as I can tell, Tara is as pure as the driven snow. I'm sure it will be a very mellow evening."

"Yeah, right," Brenna said. She stared at the paper scraps in front of her, wondering how she got into these things and, more importantly, how could she get out.

Turned out, there was no getting out of it. And so, at

eight o'clock sharp, Brenna strolled into the bar of the Fife and Drum, wearing an olive green, wool jersey sheath by Donna Karan that was sleeveless and gathered at the waist with a flattering V cut neckline.

She accessorized with peep toe, brown leather Alexander McQueen pumps and a matching clutch and had stacked several gold bangles on her right wrist. These were more of her clothes from her bygone days at the art gallery in Boston. Some of the outfits, like this dress, she just wasn't ready to give to the rummage sale—not yet anyway. Although, she was rethinking the shoes. She hadn't worn heels much since she'd been in Morse Point, and the arches in her feet were already beginning to whine in protest.

Brenna scanned the dimly lit bar until she saw Tenley. Always beautiful, she looked especially so this evening with her long blond hair up in a twist and a body-clinging, purple slip dress that made her blue eyes a startling shade of violet. She was standing amidst a crowd of younger women, looking ill at ease.

It only took a moment for Brenna to see why. One of the women was leaning over the bar, whispering in Matt Collins's ear. She was a honey-haired blonde, wearing a red-hot number by Dior that pushed her breasts up and out while flirty ruffles showed off her tan legs.

It looked to Brenna as if Tenley wanted to kick the stool right out from under the girl. She stepped up her pace across the bar.

"Brenna!" Tara greeted her with a hug and an air-kiss. She looped her arm through Brenna's and dragged her over to the group.

"This is Britney, my maid of honor," Tara said. She tapped the blonde in scorching red, who looked annoyed at having her moment with Matt interrupted.

Brenna shook her hand and watched as Tenley slid

smoothly into the spot Britney had vacated and began to chat with Matt. The young Britney looked miffed to have been supplanted and Brenna had to hide her smile.

"This is Dana," Tenley continued the introductions, "and her sister Marissa."

The sisters were a study in contrasts. While Dana was tall and thin, Marissa was short and curvy. Neither one was particularly pretty, as they both had long faces with prominent noses. They didn't strike Brenna as being happy sorts, although that could be because they both wore basic black cocktail dresses accessorized with deep, disapproving frowns.

"I still don't see why we had to get together in this godforsaken backwater," Marissa said. She looked at Brenna with absolutely no repentance. "No offense."

"None taken," Brenna said.

"Seriously," Dana said, looking at Tara. "You're really going to live here?"

"Yes," Tara said. "I think it's going to be lovely."

"I think it's going to be hell on earth," Marissa said. "There's no shopping, no theaters, no clubs. You're going to be bored out of your mind."

"Excuse me, I think I'll get a glass of wine," Brenna said before she could get dragged into the debate.

She left Tara and the grumpy sisters and squeezed in next to Tenley at the bar. Matt immediately poured her a glass of pinot grigio and she smiled her thanks.

"This is going to be a long night," she said.

"And how," Tenley agreed, with a pointed glare at Britney, who had moved down the bar to signal Matt for a refill.

"I envy Tara," Tenley said.

"Because she's getting married?" Brenna asked, taking a sip of her dry white wine.

"No, because she's marrying the man she wants and her parents are letting her."

Brenna watched her watching Matt. "You've never gotten over him, have you?"

"Is it that obvious?"

"Only to me," Brenna said. She gave her friend a reassuring squeeze. Tenley had dated Matt in high school. Her parents had forced them apart and Brenna knew her friend still suffered for it.

"There's my girl!" A shout caused them to turn around.

Jake Haywood crossed the room and swooped Tara up into a big hug. She giggled as he spun her around, and Brenna couldn't help but notice that when they looked at each other the rest of the world disappeared.

Beside Jake was his best friend, Clue Parker. Clue was the sort of guy who made the parents of pretty daughters lie awake at night worrying. He was recklessly handsome, with dark brown hair that fell over his forehead and a set of dimples bracketing his wolfish grin that were deep enough to hide spare change.

Even being a fairly new resident, Brenna knew Clue's reputation as a womanizer. She also knew that he and Jake had been friends since they were kids. Jake being the one who kept Clue from making too many bad decisions, and Clue being the one who kept Jake from making too many good ones. Like left and right, one was seldom found without the other, and she wondered how Clue was taking his best friend's upcoming wedding.

It didn't take long to find out. When Jake wasn't looking, Clue sent Tara a look of such malevolence that Brenna gasped. She looked at Tenley to see if she saw it, too, but she was busy keeping an eye on Britney and Matt. Tara was looking at Jake, and completely oblivious to anyone else, while Dana and Marissa had their heads pressed together, whispering scathing observations about the town no doubt. No one else had seen it.

When Brenna looked back at Clue, the look was gone and instead he was studying her as if he knew she'd seen him. He grinned and then licked his lips with slow deliberation. Brenna didn't know if he was hitting on her or warning her; either way it made a shiver run down her spine.

"You're not supposed to be here," Tara was chiding Jake.

"I know but I couldn't resist seeing you," he said. "Clue and I are going to the Brass Rail to shoot some pool before he starts work tonight. I want you to be careful and call me if you need a ride."

"Oh, don't worry," Tara said. "Daddy hired us a driver."

"Too bad he can't drive us out of this podunk town," Dana said with a sneer.

"Yeah, like, back to civilization," Marissa agreed.

"With faces like yours, I imagine you need a bigger pond to fish in," Clue said.

Dana gasped and Marissa huffed, while Britney laughed delightedly. In her flirty red dress, she stepped into Clue's line of sight, and his gaze raked her from head to toe. It wasn't hard to tell what he was thinking.

"That's it. I'm going home," Dana announced.

"Me, too," said Marissa.

"Oh, no, don't," Tara pleaded. "Clue was just joking, weren't you, Clue?"

He looked at her as if he had only just begun, but Jake elbowed him hard in the side. The two men stared at each other for a second and then Clue turned back to the girls.

He took each of their hands in one of his and brushed his lips across the back of Dana's and then Marissa's.

"Forgive me," he said. He flashed his dimples. "I am a complete jerk for insulting two such lovely ladies. I just can't bear the thought that you dislike Morse Point so much that you may not come back and grace us with your beauty once again."

Dana and Marissa lit up like a pair of candles at the flattery. Britney looked like she might gag, and Brenna really couldn't blame her. How the two sisters could swallow that shovelful of bull, she couldn't fathom.

"We'll leave you girls to your evening," Jake said, obviously deciding to get while the getting was good. He kissed Tara fiercely on the lips. "Call me tomorrow."

"I will," she promised with a sigh.

"I'll be at the Brass Rail all night," Clue said, stepping close to Britney. "Come by."

"I will," she promised. The innuendo oozing between them was thick enough to serve in a bowl.

"I'm hopping off this train before we make that stop," Tenley said to Brenna. "That place is a dump."

Brenna had never been in the Brass Rail, but she had heard it was a biker bar with a reputation for drug trafficking. She couldn't imagine Tara would want to go there.

After several drinks at the Fife and Drum, the party of six women took the limo Tara's father had hired to the Willow House. It was a bar/coffeehouse on the outskirts of Morse Point near the university. Both Tenley and Brenna ordered coffee, while the younger women continued with their appletinis and cosmopolitans.

By unspoken agreement, Tenley and Brenna took their coffee to a secluded table in the back. A live band was playing cover music and couples crowded the floor. Britney had found a quorum of admirers and was now dancing evocatively amidst the slack-jawed males in the center of the dance floor. Dana and Marissa hovered on the fringe of the group as if trying to bask in her reflected glory.

Tara had excused herself to take a call on her cell phone, and judging by the way her face lit up when she saw who it was, Brenna suspected it was Jake.

Both Tenley and Brenna had been asked to dance, but they declined. Tenley because she wasn't interested and Brenna because her feet were killing her, although she probably would have refused either way. The club scene just wasn't her bag.

"When did we get so old?" Tenley shouted over the music, as if reading her mind.

"I don't think we're old," Brenna said. "It's just that we've done all this before. Who wants their life to be a rerun?"

"Good point," Tenley said. And then she giggled and asked, "Are you as tired as I am?"

"Yes," Brenna said and then she giggled, too. "My God, we are old!"

A tall man wearing an expensive suit approached their table. He carried himself with a distinct sense of purpose and the raw power he exuded was impossible to ignore. Brenna prepared to politely rebuff the man's advance when recognition struck.

"Dom!" She broke into a grin.

"Ladies." He leaned down and kissed each of their cheeks. Then he stood back and glowered at Brenna.

"You never returned my call," he said.

"I'm sorry," she said. "I meant to, but after the funeral, well, everything just got away from me."

"I understand," he said.

His chocolate brown eyes were warm with empathy, and Brenna wished, not for the first time, that they made her feel the same zip that Nate's did.

"Join us?" Tenley asked, and Dom pulled out a chair and sat with them.

They had met Dom Cappicola, the son of a mobster, several months ago when they were conducting some amateur sleuthing, trying to clear Nate of a bogus murder charge.

Dom had let his interest in Brenna be known, but with her feelings toward Nate all in a muddle, she didn't think it was fair to Dom to encourage him. Still, he was attractive and at any other time she might have felt differently, especially since he was trying to turn the Cappicola family business legit.

"How are things in Morse Point since the mayor's murderer was locked up?" he asked.

"Back to normal," Tenley said. "Well, as normal as anything is in Morse Point."

"What brings you up from Bayview?" Brenna asked.

"My nephew," Dom said with a sigh. He pointed to a gangly youth on the dance floor with Britney. He wore a shiny suit open enough at the throat to display an array of gold chains. He looked like a gangster wannabe. "He's been having some issues with the law."

"Oh," Brenna said. She wasn't sure she wanted to know more. She knew some members of Dom's family were less than thrilled with the direction he was taking the family business in since his father's retirement, and she wondered if the nephew was one of them.

Britney glanced over at their table and her eyes narrowed when she saw Dom. Just like that, she began to work her way toward their table, walking like a supermodel on the catwalk. Dom failed to notice her, however, and Brenna had to look down to keep herself from smiling when Britney's face went from seductive tart to miffed debutante.

Seeing his nephew heading for the door, Dom rose from his seat to follow.

"Looks like I'm off," he said with a wry grin.

"Good to see you," Tenley said.

"You, too," Dom said. He had unintentionally turned his back to Britney, who did not look pleased at being ignored. He leaned close to Brenna and said, "Just so we're clear, I'm going to ask you officially, may I take you out sometime?"

"Oh," Brenna said. She knew she sounded stupid, but being totally caught off guard, she didn't know what else to say. To Dom's credit, he grinned at her.

"Surprised you, didn't I?" he asked.

"A little," she admitted.

"Well?" he asked.

She glanced around them in a blatant stall maneuver. Britney was almost at their table. Tenley was pretending that she wasn't listening when Brenna knew full well that she was. She felt herself grow warm with embarrassment, which was ridiculous. It was a simple question.

Yes, she had a crush on Nate, but Nate wasn't asking her out and Dom was and under any other circumstance, she would probably like Dom very much.

"Okay," she said. "Yes."

He blinked. She'd surprised him, which made her smile.

"All right then, I'll be calling." He gave her a quick kiss on the mouth, which was warm and tasted faintly of coffee. He gazed at her for a moment and then said, "In case I neglected to tell you, you look beautiful tonight."

"Thanks," Brenna said. Her voice sounded hoarse, which made his smile deepen.

She watched him leave, feeling Tenley's gaze on the side of her face. When she sensed Tenley was about to speak, she raised her hand and said, "Don't say a word."

"Word." Tenley ignored her with a chortle.

"Who was that?" Britney demanded, arriving at their table.

"Brenna's boyfriend," Tenley said.

"Just a friend," Brenna said.

"For now," Tenley sang.

Tara and the grumpy sisters joined them, and Tenley said, "Well, ladies, I think it is time to call it a night."

Britney glanced at her delicate, diamond-encrusted Cartier wristwatch. "But it's just after midnight."

"See? We'd better go before we all turn into pumpkins," Brenna said. She and Tenley rose, giving the girls no choice but to follow.

"Remember, Tara," Brenna said. "We're meeting your mother at the shop at nine."

"I'm never going to make it," Tara said with a hiccup. She wobbled on her spindly heels, and Brenna could tell she'd had too much to drink.

"Tell you what," Brenna said, taking her elbow to help her navigate the gravel driveway. "I'll pick you up on my way in tomorrow to make sure you're on time."

"Oh, would you?" Tara asked. "See? I just knew we were going to be the best of friends."

Brenna didn't have the heart to tell her that she was only doing it because she didn't want to face Tara's mother by herself.

The women piled into the limo in a clumsy heap while Tenley asked the driver to bring them back to the Fife and Drum where she and Brenna had left their cars. The visiting girls all had rooms at the Morse Point Inn, an old Victorian house in the center of town that had been remodeled to accommodate guests. Tara, meanwhile, was renting the Crawford bungalow. Brenna knew this because the Porter twins had mentioned that she lived two houses down from them every day since the day she moved in.

As the driver wound his way back toward the center of town, Dana turned on the stereo inside the limo. Pink burst out of the speakers, singing about getting the party started. Brenna found that ironic since all she wanted to do was take off her shoes and go to bed.

The limo pulled up in front of the Fife and Drum and Brenna gratefully stepped out when the driver held the door open. She took a deep breath of the sweet night air, as if she were a felon being paroled. Tenley followed, looking as relieved as Brenna felt.

Tara was about to step out as well, as her bungalow was easily within walking distance, but Britney looped an arm about her friend's waist and pulled her back into the car and slammed the door.

Tenley and Brenna exchanged a glance, and then Britney's, and Tara's heads popped up out of the sunroof on the limo looking like a two-headed jack-in-the-box.

"Woo hoo!" Britney yelled. "Driver, to the Brass Rail!"

The man hurried back around the car and got into the driver's seat.

"Oh, I really think I should call it a night," Tara said.

"Don't be such a party pooper!" Britney snapped. "I came all this way to go out with you and the night isn't even half over."

Tara bit her lip, obviously trying to decide between common sense and accommodating her friend. The friend won, and Tara nodded in a sleepy, drunken way.

"Brenna, promise to wake me up tomorrow!" she called as she lurched against the roof when the limo began to pull away from the curb.

"I promise!" Brenna called with a wave, relieved that she had escaped when she did.

"I'll bet you fifty bucks, she regrets that decision tomorrow," Tenley said.

"And how," Brenna agreed.

A nudge against her hip roused Brenna from her sleep. She would have ignored it, but given that she'd been sleeping alone for the past few years, it was hard to ignore the presence of another being in her bed.

She opened one eye and found herself nose to muzzle

with Hank. He had his head on the pillow beside hers, looking as content as if he'd just corralled a field full of rabbits.

Brenna glanced at the clock. It was seven thirty. She was to meet Tiffany at the shop at nine and if she was going to pick up Tara first, she'd better get moving.

Grateful that she hadn't had much to drink the night before, Brenna took Hank for a quick jog around their corner of the lake. Then it was a fast shower and into the Jeep for the four and a half mile ride into town.

She drove with her windows down, letting the cool morning air flirt with her hair and sweep across her skin, leaving goose bumps in its wake.

She pulled up in front of Tara's bungalow, a square light blue house with white trim and a narrow porch. She glanced at the clock on her dashboard. It was quarter to nine. She fervently hoped that Tara was up and moving. She did not relish the idea of trying to hose a drunk girl off in the shower.

She rapped on Tara's door, but there was no response. *Shocker.*

She tried the doorknob, and much to her dismay, it opened. What was this girl thinking? Having been the victim of a nasty robbery in Boston, Brenna took her personal safety very seriously and was mystified when others, especially other women, did not. Maybe she was paranoid and saw a bad guy lurking around every corner, but it kept her safe and nowadays that seemed like a good plan to her.

She knocked on the doorframe, hoping to rouse Tara without having to go inside. There was no answer. She did three more sharp raps and yelled, "Hello?"

Still, no answer. Feeling like an intruder herself, she stepped into Tara's small house. It was quiet. There was no sound of the shower running or anyone snoring. Maybe Tara had left already.

Still, she felt that she ought to check. She walked through the narrow living room, where a rounded love seat and armchair were decorated in a pretty cobalt blue and white floral upholstery. Stacks of wedding magazines littered the glass coffee table, underneath which the shoes Tara had been wearing the night before lay discarded.

A breakfast bar separated the kitchenette, which was clean and painted bright yellow. Beyond that was a short hallway with two doors; one led to an empty bathroom and the other was half closed. It had to be the bedroom.

"Tara? It's Brenna, are you up yet?" Brenna took a deep breath and pushed open the door. She really hoped to find the bed made and Tara gone, having left in such a hurry she forgot to lock her door. But no.

The smell struck her first, a metallic odor that bit at her nostrils, causing her to recoil. Something was very wrong. She saw the rumpled bed next. Two heads were visible above the bunched-up purple comforter, one blond and one dark brown.

Oh, gees! Tara wasn't alone, and unless Brenna missed her guess the head beside hers did not belong to Jake. She thought about just leaving, but then she feared Tiffany would come storming in here and that made her feel badly for Tara.

"Oh for Pete's sake!" Brenna snapped, annoyed. She stomped toward the bed. She would wake Tara and then let her deal with the disaster she'd created.

Tara was sound asleep with her mouth hanging open and her skin a pasty shade of gray. Brenna gently shook her, but she was nonresponsive. She wondered if she should douse her with ice water, but she didn't want to wake Tara's companion and have to bear witness to that.

She shook Tara again and hissed, "Tara, wake up!"

The bedclothes slid off of her shoulder, and Brenna stepped back with a gasp. Clutched in Tara's right hand was a long, lethal-looking serrated kitchen knife, and it was covered in blood.

Chapter 4

"Wha... huh?" Tara mumbled. Her eyes cracked open a little and then she shifted as if she were going to roll over on the knife.

"Tara, wake up!" Brenna yelled. She lunged forward and grabbed Tara's shoulder to keep her from stabbing herself.

"Brenna?" Tara blinked at her. "Oh, no, did I oversleep? I'm sorry."

Brenna ran her eyes over the young woman, looking for any signs of injury. Tara was wearing a thin pale blue nightdress. It had several blood smears on it, but she couldn't find any gashes or open wounds on Tara. So where had the blood come from? Brenna glanced over Tara at the body beside her.

"Tara, what happened last night?" she asked.

Tara looked down at her hands and saw the knife she still held. She jumped and dropped it. She ran her hands over her gown and saw the brown stains, then she looked up at Brenna with confused eyes.

"What is this?" she asked.

"Blood," Brenna said.

"Whose?"

"His?" Brenna guessed, pointing behind Tara to the body beyond.

Tara whipped her head around, saw the man in her bed, let out an ear-piercing shriek, and leapt out of the bed.

"Oh, my God, who is that?"

"You don't know?" Brenna asked.

"No, I . . . wait, why did I have a knife in my hand?" she asked.

Her blue eyes were huge, the pupils tiny, and she was so pale, she looked as if all of the blood had been drained out of her. She swayed on her feet and Brenna was afraid she'd faint. She put an arm around her and led her to a chair in the corner.

"I'm going to see if I can rouse him," Brenna said. "Wait here."

She circled the bed to the other side. The man was lying with his face buried in the pillows. His dark hair covered the side of his face, and all she could see was his bare shoulder peeking out above the fluffy purple covers.

"Ahem, excuse me, sir," she said. She reached forward and prodded his shoulder with the heel of her hand.

He didn't respond and he felt unnaturally stiff. Brenna stared at the covers; they weren't moving, as in he wasn't breathing. Panic hit her like a fist in the chest.

She prodded his shoulder again. No response. She felt Tara walk up behind her.

"What's wrong?" she asked.

"I don't think he's breathing," Brenna said. "I'm going to try and turn him over."

She hunkered down beside the bed, and using both hands pushed his shoulder up and over. It was like trying to lift a car. With a grunt, she gave him a shove and he flopped over.

It was then that she saw the wounds on his forearms and the huge, gaping hole in his chest. It was Clue Parker, and he was dead.

Tara let out another earsplitting scream, and Brenna turned and pulled the girl into her arms. She was shaking and gasping and Brenna feared she was beginning to hyperventilate. She half carried, half dragged Tara into the kitchen, where she pushed her onto a stool while she foraged for a paper bag.

Finding one in the third drawer, she shook it open and held it out to Tara. "Breathe into this."

Tara did as she was told while Brenna reached for the phone and called 9-1-1. She could imagine what Chief Barker was going to say when he arrived to find she had discovered another body.

The chief was not happy to see her. He had Brenna and Tara stay in the small living room while he went to the bedroom to check on Clue. When he came back his face was set in grim lines.

The medical examiner was on the way, and Officer DeFalco, the chief's right-hand man, was busy putting up yellow crime scene tape all around the small bungalow. Brenna knew it was only a matter of minutes before the entire town knew.

"What's going on?"

"Is someone hurt?"

Make that seconds, Brenna thought. She turned and saw the two gray heads peering through the open door and sighed.

Marie and Ella were even faster than she had anticipated.

"Brenna!" Ella called as she spied her in the corner of
the room. "What's going on?"

"Is it that Montgomery girl?" Marie asked. "Was she
robbed? Is she hurt?"

Officer DeFalco stepped in front of them, blocking their
view into the house. Undeterred, the two ladies hunched
down and stared at Brenna under his outstretched arms.

"Was she assaulted?" Ella said the words in a gasp.

"Was it sexual?" Marie whispered.

"Ladies!" DeFalco barked. "Back up and move away
from the house. We have crime scene personnel coming
that need to get through."

"Crime scene!" the two ladies said together.

DeFalco looked like he wanted to throttle them. Instead he took them each by an elbow and trotted them to
the curb.

"Do not put one toe on this property," he warned. "Or I
will take you in for obstruction of justice."

"Humph," Marie sniffed.

"Well, I never," Ella huffed.

They looked suitably miffed, but Brenna noticed that
neither of them came any closer to the house.

Chief Barker was questioning Tara in the spare bedroom, and Brenna paced while she waited for him to talk
to her. She knew he was going to want a full accounting
of this morning's events.

She hoped she could remember it all, but it had already
begun to blur in her mind. She was still reeling from the
shock of finding Clue in Tara's bed. Had Tara been fool-
ing around on Jake with his best friend?

It seemed completely out of character for the young
bride. Brenna had been so sure that Tara was madly in
love with Jake. Why would she have an affair? And why

would she stab Clue? Had he threatened to tell Jake? It seemed the most likely answer, but still improbable given what Brenna knew about Tara.

Chief Barker brought Tara back into the living room. She sank onto the sofa, her face splotchy from crying and her eyes red-rimmed and swollen.

"Brenna, I'd like to speak to you," he said.

"Sure," she said. She felt like she should have words of comfort for Tara, but she had no idea what to say.

"Chief, the medical examiner is here," DeFalco called from the door.

"I'll be right back," he said to Brenna.

She nodded.

She knew this was going to take a while. She took the seat beside Tara and asked, "Are you all right? Can I get you anything?"

Tara blinked at her. She was the picture of misery.

"Jake can't find out," she said.

"About Clue?" Brenna asked. "I don't see how he won't find out that his best friend is dead."

"He can't find out that he was in my bed," Tara said. "He'll misunderstand. He'll never forgive me."

"Misunderstand what?" Brenna asked. "Tara, did you sleep with Clue?"

"No!" she wailed. She looked away from Brenna toward the door where gloved crime scene personnel began to file into the house. "I don't know. I can't remember."

She crumpled into a heap of sobs and Brenna put her arms around her shoulders. She believed Tara. The look of confusion in her eyes was genuine. She must have had so much to drink that she blacked out. There was no telling what had happened between her and Clue.

Brenna had seen the look of malevolence in Clue's eyes the night before at the bar. He had been angry that his friend was getting married; of that she was certain.

Had he been so angry that he did the unthinkable? Had he attacked Tara, giving her no choice but to defend herself? If so, why couldn't she remember any of it?

"That's my daughter in there. I demand that you let me through this instant," a voice snapped from the door.

Tiffany Montgomery stood there, going nose to nose with Officer DeFalco.

"Mother!" Tara called. She bolted up from the sofa and ran across the room. DeFalco was forced to step aside as Tara threw herself into her mother's arms.

"Baby," Tiffany crooned into her daughter's hair. "Are you all right?"

Tara wept and Tiffany held her, letting her daughter sob into her Chanel suit.

"Ms. Montgomery." Chief Barker reappeared, with a female officer. "This is Investigator Wheatley. She needs to take your nightgown for testing."

Mrs. Montgomery looked outraged, but the chief cut her off. "Feel free to call your attorney, but this is the scene of a murder and we will be treating it as such. Brenna?"

Leaving the Montgomery women with the female investigator, Chief Barker gestured for Brenna to follow him into the spare room.

He looked at her as if he wasn't sure what to say. Brenna knew that he had to be thinking that there had been two bodies found in Morse Point in the past three months and she had been the one to find them both. It was even more eventful given that the town hadn't had a murder in fifty years.

"So, here we are again," Brenna said.

The chief had a thick gray mustache that he rubbed with the side of his index finger when he was thinking. He did that now.

"Tell me what happened," he said. "And don't leave anything out."

Brenna took a deep breath and told him everything she could remember. She tried not to get emotional but she knew she blanched when she talked about finding Clue dead.

"You were the first one here," Barker said. "Was there any sign of a forced entry?"

"No, the door was shut but not locked," Brenna said. "I remember thinking how unsafe that was."

"Was the house in order? Did anything strike you as odd?" he asked.

"Only that she was asleep and we were to meet her mother at the shop in a few minutes," she said. "That's why I tried to wake her up, even when I realized there was someone else in the bed, too. I didn't want her mother to walk in and find her like that."

Chief Barker had taken out a pad and was making notes. He considered Brenna for a moment. "You know, people are going to talk."

"Well, yeah," Brenna agreed. "I mean, no matter how it happened, Clue was in bed with his best friend's fiancée."

"No, I meant about you," Chief Barker said. "Two bodies in three months is grist for the gossip mill."

Brenna wanted to argue. It wasn't her fault she had been in the wrong place at the wrong time twice, but she knew it would sound lame.

"I suppose," she said.

"I just wanted to give you a heads-up," he said. "You're free to go, but I want you to call me if you remember anything else, and I may have more questions for you as the case progresses. Otherwise, you are to steer clear of this investigation. Understood?"

Brenna nodded. She knew the drill.

They left the bedroom to find Tara's mother blasting one of the medical examiner's people.

"You will not touch my daughter, not one hand upon her person, do you understand?"

Chief Barker hurried across the room. Brenna took in the sight of Tiffany standing in front of a forlorn Tara.

"We will happily wait for your attorney," Chief Barker said, his voice low and soothing. "But we do need to take some blood and hair samples, and we'll use a subpoena if we have to."

"Let me through, DeFalco," a voice said at the door. "I'll either go around you or through you, but make no mistake I'm coming in."

"It's Jake!" Tara clutched her mother's arm. "Please, he can't find me like this."

Chapter 5

"Tara!" Jake yelled.

"No, don't come in," Tara cried.

"Talk to me, Tara. What's going on?" he said.

Jake was trying to get around Officer DeFalco, who was holding on to the doorframe in a remarkable impression of a brick wall, refusing to budge.

"Nothing," she said. Her voice was too weak to give the lie any substance and Jake knew it. He bobbed and weaved around DeFalco, looking for an opening.

"Jake, this is a police matter." Chief Barker stepped up behind his officer. "I'm going to ask you to leave."

"You're going to have to haul me away," Jake said. "I'm not leaving until I see Tara and know that she's okay."

The chief let out a sigh and turned to face Tara. She was standing behind her mother and shook her head frantically from side to side.

"No," she whispered. "He can't see me like this."

"Send him away," Tiffany demanded.

"Don't do it, Tara," Brenna said. Everyone turned to look at her, and she cleared her throat. She stepped closer and said, "Morse Point is a very small town. He is going to find out what happened, probably in the next ten minutes. Don't you think it's better if it comes from you?"

"What will I tell him?" she asked.

"The truth," Brenna said.

Tara's blue eyes searched Brenna's. She was looking for reassurance that it was going to be okay. Brenna wished she could give her that; instead she gave her sympathy.

Tara stepped out from behind her mother and straightened her shoulders. She had changed into jeans and a T-shirt. Her feet were bare and her hair was still mussed from sleep. She looked tiny and vulnerable but resolved.

"Okay, then," she said. She turned to Chief Barker. "Can I see him?"

"With me present," Chief Barker said.

"All right," Tara agreed.

"Let him in," Barker ordered.

DeFalco stepped aside and Jake all but fell into the room. He hurried across the room and snatched Tara into his arms.

"Oh, thank God, you're safe," he said as he buried kisses in her hair. "The Porter sisters showed up at the garage. They said you'd had a break-in and that the police were here, and they feared you'd been assaulted. Are you okay, baby?"

"I'm fine," Tara said. She hugged him close, and Brenna saw her eyes close as she pressed herself against the full length of him. She looked as if she were trying to memorize the feel of him.

After a long moment, she stepped back. "Jake, I have some bad news."

"What?" he asked. Then he gave a sideways glance at Tiffany, who was standing with her arms wrapped around

her middle as if she felt her daughter's pain all the way to
her bone marrow. "Are you calling off the wedding?"

Tara gave him a weak smile. "I'd never do that."

He sagged with relief.

"But, Jake," she said, her voice hoarse with emotion,
"Clue is dead."

"Clue?" Jake asked. He looked confused. "How? I
don't understand. Was there an accident?"

Tara bit her lip. It seemed as if everyone in the room
had gone still, their attention focused upon her. She raised
her hands in a helpless gesture.

"I don't know," she said.

Jake looked at her and then her mother. His gaze
skipped over Brenna and he turned to face Chief Barker.

"What's going on, Chief?" he said. He sounded more
authoritative than his years would warrant.

"We're trying to figure that out," Chief Barker said.

When he didn't explain any further, Brenna realized he
considered Jake a suspect. It made sense. If Jake had
come here and found Clue in bed with his girl, he very
well could have been the one to kill his friend.

Brenna saw the confusion flit across Jake's face. She
didn't think he was faking. He really had no idea what
was going on.

"I'd like to ask you some questions, Jake," Chief Barker
said. "If you'll follow me?"

He led Jake back into the guest bedroom. On the way they
passed Tara's room, where the crime scene personnel were
still working on Clue. Jake's footsteps faltered as he took in
the scene and recognized his friend in his fiancée's bed.

He spun around to face Tara. His face was ravaged by
shock and outrage.

"In your bed? My friend is in your bed?" he shouted.

"I can explain," Tara said. "Please don't look at me like
that. There's been a mistake."

Jake made to cross the room to her, but Barker restrained him with a hand on his arm.

"No, Jake," he said. "I need to question you first."

"But she and he . . ." He gestured toward the bedroom. "What the hell happened here last night? Did you sleep with him? Did you sleep with my best friend?"

His voice was a savage growl, and Tara recoiled from him even as her mother stepped forward, putting herself between them.

"Not now, Jake." Chief Barker tightened his hold on him and forcibly pulled him into the other room. The door slammed shut.

Tara began to sob in earnest and Tiffany pulled her into her arms. "I don't know what happened, Mother. How can I reassure him when I don't know myself?"

"You didn't do anything wrong," Tiffany said as she pulled back to look at her daughter's face. "I'm calling your father. He'll know what to do."

She fished her cell phone out of her purse and pressed a few buttons. She walked into the kitchenette to have what little privacy the bungalow afforded.

Tara's red-rimmed eyes met Brenna's. She was the picture of misery, and Brenna remembered when she had been in a similarly bad situation, the victim of a robbery in Boston. She crossed the room and took Tara's hands in hers.

"It's going to be all right," she said. "Chief Barker is very good at what he does. He'll find out what happened and catch whoever did this horrible thing."

"What if it was me?" Tara's voice was barely a whisper, but Brenna heard her and felt the cold fingers of dread creep up her spine.

"Move aside!" Mr. Montgomery ordered. "That's my girl in there."

"Daddy!" Tara rushed to the door and threw herself into her father's arms.

Mr. Montgomery was tall and broad with thinning gray hair. He was wearing a golf shirt and khaki pants as if he had been called on his way to the links.

Mr. Montgomery held his daughter tight and glanced over her head at his wife. She met his gaze and in a gesture reminiscent of her daughter she bit her lip as if she didn't know what to say.

"It's okay, honey," he said. "Daddy's here. I'll take care of everything."

Tara stepped back and wiped her streaming eyes with the back of her hand.

"You can't, Daddy," she sobbed. "No one can."

The door to the guest bedroom banged open and crashed against the wall. Jake stormed out with two patches of angry scarlet staining his cheeks. He stopped in front of Tara and glared at her.

"Jake . . ." She reached out a hand to him, but he shrugged it off and stomped to the door.

"I'm late for work," he said to no one in particular.

DeFalco stepped aside as if he expected Jake would plow him over if he didn't move fast enough.

Tara buried her face in her hands and sobbed while Mr. Montgomery blustered at the chief.

"What is the meaning of this?"

"This is a criminal investigation," Chief Barker said.

"My daughter has done nothing wrong."

"Then she has nothing to worry about," Barker said.

"I am taking her out of this backwater and back to Boston where she belongs," her father announced. "Tara, get your things. We're leaving."

Tara sobbed even louder, and her mother pulled her protectively against her.

"I'm afraid I can't let you do that," Chief Barker said. "There is a dead man in the next room and she was found holding the knife. I'm going to have to take her in and we'll see what a judge has to say about her release."

"I'm calling my attorney," Mr. Montgomery said.

"That would be wise," Chief Barker agreed. He nodded at Officer DeFalco, and Brenna realized he hadn't been standing in the doorway to keep people out as much as he had been to keep Tara in.

"If you'll go peacefully with Officer DeFalco, Miss Montgomery, we'll forgo the handcuffs," Chief Barker said.

Mr. and Mrs. Montgomery looked horrified as their baby girl was escorted outside to a waiting squad car.

"You haven't heard the last from me, Barker," Montgomery said.

"See you at the station," the chief said.

He and Brenna watched as the Montgomerys hurried to their Lexus and fell in line behind the police car as it left the curb.

"What's going to happen to her?" Brenna asked. She couldn't help thinking of her own unfortunate experience with the Boston PD a few years before.

"It won't be like what you went through," Chief Barker said. He had an uncanny ability to read her mind. "She's innocent until proven guilty. That said, it would be really helpful if she could remember what happened last night."

"Maybe it will come to her when she gets over the shock," Brenna suggested.

"Maybe," he said. He sounded doubtful. "I hear Nate is out of town and you're babysitting Hank."

"Just for a few days," she said.

"Where did he go?"

Brenna glanced at him. Surely, he didn't think that Nate had anything to do with last night's events. Just because he had been the prime suspect in the mayor's murder a few months ago didn't mean he was involved in this mess.

"I'm just curious," he said. Again, giving Brenna the sense that he knew what she'd been thinking.

"He didn't say," she said. "Just that he'd be back in a few days."

"Chief," the medical examiner called from the back bedroom. "Can you come here?"

"I'll let you go," Brenna said quickly.

"If you think of anything else . . ." he began, and Brenna finished, "I'll let you know."

She watched as he walked toward the bedroom. She could see several crime scene technicians gathering samples from around the room and the shock hit her all over again. Even now, hours later, she had a hard time wrapping her brain around the fact that Clue Parker had been found dead in Tara's bed.

"Then what happened?" Tenley asked.

Brenna and Tenley were decoupaging a cedar hope chest for Betty Cartwright. She lived in the senior housing complex on the edge of town and had her eye on an eligible bachelor there.

She had commissioned Brenna to make the chest for her in the belief that by being a proactive optimist and having a hope chest ready to be filled, she'd get her man.

The chest had begun as bare wood, so the process was from the bones out. Brenna had coated it with paint primer, sanded it, and painted it a deep burning yellow. Now she and Tenley were using a print of *The Kiss* by Gustav Klimt, which they had cut into small two-inch squares and were now gluing onto the chest like a mosaic, leaving groutlike lines of the yellow wood visible between the papers.

They were only halfway done, but Brenna was pleased with the outcome so far. Betty had been excited by the idea and Brenna hoped she was as happy with the finished result.

She used a brayer, a handheld rubber roller, to flatten what she had just glued on while Tenley prepped more of the paper squares.

"Well?" Tenley prodded.

"Oh, sorry," Brenna said. She put the brayer aside and looked at her friend. "Let's see. Jake stormed from the house, Tara got taken to the station by Officer DeFalco, her parents followed, and then Chief Barker and I talked about Nate."

"Nate?" Tenley asked. "Why?"

"He wanted to know if I knew where he'd gone," Brenna said.

"Surely, he doesn't think he's a suspect," Tenley said.

"No, but I thought the same thing," Brenna said. "He said he was just curious, but now that I think about it, I bet it has something to do with fishing."

The two men were known for daylong fishing trips that always ended with stories of the big one that got away.

"Do you think Tara did it?" Tenley asked.

"No—I don't know—no," Brenna said.

"Choose one," Tenley said.

"No," Brenna said. "I saw her face when she saw him in her bed. She was shocked. If she'd killed him, surely she would have remembered it on some level."

"You'd think," Tenley agreed.

The front door opened and both women looked up. The Porter sisters had arrived and were striding across the room, trying to elbow each other out of the way in their desire to get to Brenna.

Tenley hurried forward to save her display of Durwin Rice's *New Decoupage* book, which was hip-checked by Ella as she pushed past Marie.

"What do you know?" Ella demanded, sitting across the table from Brenna.

"What was Clue Parker doing in Tara Montgomery's house? Was he really in her bed?" Marie asked as she plunked down next to her sister.

Brenna raised an eyebrow and studied the two sisters. When they were on a quest for information, they had all the finesse of a pair of truffle pigs. In fact, she was pretty sure she saw their nostrils flaring now. They were relentless.

"What can I tell you that you don't already know?" she asked.

"Were they having an affair?" Ella asked.

"I don't know," Brenna said. Ella frowned.

"Do you think Jake killed Clue in a jealous rage?" Marie asked. Her eyes glowed as if she thought the idea romantic. Brenna frowned.

"I don't know."

"Well, what *do* you know?" they asked in unison.

"Clue was stabbed. He was found in Tara's bed. She didn't appear to remember anything," she said. "And that's all I know."

"Humph," Ella snorted, as if she thought Brenna was holding out on them.

"There, there, dear," Marie said as she reached out and patted Brenna's hand. "You're just not as experienced as we are at fact gathering. It's an art, you know."

Tenley rejoined them and Brenna noticed that she quickly ducked her head as if to stifle a laugh.

"Well, I think she did it," Ella declared. "She's not from around here, and you know what those young women from Boston are like, loose morals and such. He probably threatened to tell Jake and she ran a knife right through his poor heart."

"I'm sorry, but I really don't see how her not being from around here makes her likely to commit murder,"

Brenna said. She knew she sounded snippy, but sheesh, she wasn't from around here either.

"Oh, now I've offended you," Ella said. "Brenna, you know you're different."

"Different how?" she asked. "I don't have loose morals? How do you know?"

"Well, you're friends with Tenley," Ella said as if it were the most obvious thing in the world. "She's a daughter of the founding family. You can't get a higher recommendation than that."

"That's the second time you've told me that," Brenna said. She turned to face Tenley and said, "Could you please commit a lewd and lascivious act and ruin your reputation so that you are on the same level with the rest of us mortals?"

"Hmm. And give up my goddess status?" Tenley asked. "I don't know."

"It wouldn't change a thing," Marie said. "She's still a Morse. Having Tenley as a friend does speak well for you, my dear."

"Well, thank you, Tenley," Brenna said.

"Don't mention it," Tenley said with a dismissive wave of her hand. Her mouth was quirked up in the corner and Brenna knew she was teasing.

"Oh, look at the time," Marie declared with a glance at her watch. "We have to go, Sister. Kim Lebrowski is getting off her shift at the hospital and she went to school with Jake and Clue. Maybe she knows something."

Ella perched the handles of her wicker purse on her elbow and said, "Good call. Let's go. We'll see you ladies at class tomorrow night."

They left as abruptly as they arrived, leaving Brenna and Tenley staring after them.

"That reminds me," Brenna said. "I need to prep tomorrow night's project."

"What were you thinking?" Tenley asked.

"I don't know yet," Brenna said. "But I think I'll hold off on finishing the glass plates. I feel like we should wait until we know if Tara will be joining us again to finish hers."

Tenley nodded in understanding. She had a delicate profile, much like Tara's, and Brenna was struck by the similarity between the two women. Both were young and blond and very kind, both came from wealthy families; but where Tenley's family was aloof and frequently unforgiving, Tara's family rallied around her. Brenna couldn't even imagine how the Morse family would react if Tenley were found in bed with her fiancé's dead best friend. It wouldn't be pretty.

Her mind flashed on Clue and she remembered the stiffness of his body at her touch, the gaping wound in his chest, the metallic smell of his blood. A shudder rippled through her. Who had hated him so much that they felt compelled to stab him right through the heart?

"I wish I knew more about Clue Parker," she said.

"What?" Tenley asked. "Why?"

"Because I don't think Tara did it," she said. "I think it had to be someone who hated him or maybe feared him."

"How does that have anything to do with you?" Tenley asked.

"You heard the Porter sisters. Just because Tara isn't from around here, she's suspect number one."

"She was also found in bed with the dead guy," Tenley pointed out. "It doesn't look good."

"I know that, but I also know what it's like to be wrongly accused," Brenna said. "And I just can't bear to stand idly by and do nothing."

"Chief Barker is going to be so unhappy about this," Tenley said.

"Who said we have to tell him?" Brenna asked.

"Obviously, you have not lived here long enough," Tenley said. "Believe me, he'll find out."

"So what if he does?" Brenna asked. "I was there this morning. I'm the one who found them. I'm telling you, Tara was shocked. I really don't think she did it, and I'm going to help prove it."

"How?"

"By talking to the people who knew Clue the best," Brenna said. "His ex-girlfriends."

Chapter 6

"Well, that narrows it to half of the county," Tenley said.

Brenna rose from her seat. Tenley had a point. She had forgotten what a womanizer Clue had been.

She gathered her bowl of water and glue brushes and put them in the sink in the break room. Then she collected the remaining paper cutouts and carefully tucked them into a manila folder that she stored in the bottom drawer of her faux Louis the XIV armoire.

The bells jangled on the front door and in walked Matt Collins, the bartender at the Fife and Drum, and an old high school flame of Tenley's.

He was tall with broad shoulders and frequently wore his sleeves shoved up past his elbows as if it were a habit to keep them dry from the bar. His thick blond hair was tousled as if the wind had run its fingers through it on his way over to Vintage Papers.

"Afternoon, Brenna, Tenley," he said. He looked more at home popping in here than he had a few months ago. He'd been instrumental in helping Brenna find the mayor's killer, and Brenna had come to view him as a friend. Judging by the way Tenley lit up at the sight of him, however, she had more than friendship on her mind.

"Just the person I wanted to see," Brenna said.

"Really?" he asked.

"Yes, can you help me lift this chest onto the floor?" she asked.

"So, you're just after my muscle," he said.

"Yeah, pretty much," she said.

He gave a put-upon sigh, which was ruined by his grin. They each took a side and hefted the chest off the worktable and shuffle-walked it over to a spot by the wall to dry.

"This is going to be really nice," he said. "Miss Cartwright might land her man yet."

"I hope so," Tenley said. "She's such a character. I'd like to see her happy."

"It's hard to change the ways of a confirmed bachelor, though," Brenna said. She was hoping to lead Matt into a discussion about Clue's love life.

"That's true," he agreed. "There's a lot to recommend the single life."

"What if a guy meets the right girl?" Tenley asked.

Brenna gave her a look, but Tenley's attention was focused on Matt. Brenna got the feeling she was fishing, but not for the information Brenna wanted. Rather, she was inquiring for herself. Well, that wasn't helpful at all!

Brenna cleared her throat to bring Matt's attention back to her. "For example, I'm sure Clue Parker would have found his mate for life—eventually."

Both Tenley and Matt looked at her.

"What?" she asked. "Not subtle enough?"

They exchanged a look that said they found her both amusing and worrisome.

"Brenna, truthfully, I came here because I knew you

were the one who found Clue, and I wanted to know how
you're doing," Matt said. "But now I'm getting the feeling
that you are up to something."

"Me?" Brenna asked. She batted her eyelashes as inno-
cently as she could. Matt didn't look like he was buying
it. "Oh, all right, who was Clue Parker dating?"

"Why do you want to know?"

"Because I am sticking my nose where it doesn't belong."

"Good, so long as we're all clear on that," Matt said.

"You may as well have a seat," Tenley offered. "She's
not going to let you go until she gets what she wants."

Matt took a seat at the table and Brenna sat across from
him. Tenley went to the break room and came back with a
pot of coffee and three mugs.

As they fussed with their cream and sugar, Matt studied Brenna. "What does Nate have to say about you looking into the murder?"

"Nothing," Brenna said.

"Nothing because he doesn't know, or nothing because
you told him to mind his own beeswax?"

"He's out of town for a few days," she conceded. "Not
that it matters."

"Uh-huh," Matt said. "Why are you so interested in this
murder?"

"Because I was there," Brenna said.

"Try again," Matt said.

"He's very clever," Brenna said to Tenley, who nodded
and said, "I know."

"Flattery will get you nowhere," Matt said, but Brenna
could tell he was pleased.

She decided to put all of her cards on the table. "Okay.
I don't think Tara did it, but I do think she will get blamed
because she's not from around here, and I want to see if I
can help."

"We're not that narrow-minded," Matt said.

Brenna just looked at him. Tenley coughed into her fist.

"Oh, all right, some townspeople might be narrower than others," he said. He took a long sip from his coffee. "You know Clue was working his way through every bedroom in town."

"Not mine," Tenley said. They both looked at her. "I just wanted that clear."

Matt grinned at her, and Brenna had to stifle the urge to groan.

"Ahem, yes, well," she said to get his attention. "Was there anyone he had any sort of a relationship with?"

"A few lasted longer than others," he said. "Bonnie Jeffries from the post office was his first real love, but she dumped him when he cheated on her with her mother."

Brenna and Tenley both winced at the same time.

"Then there was Lisa Sutton," Tenley said. "Remember, they used to circle the town green on his motorcycle until Mayor Ripley threatened to have it impounded for violating the noise ordinance."

"Yeah, but she ran off to be a chef in Boston," Matt said. "He did go with Julie Harper for a while."

Brenna sat up. "Julie over at the salon?"

"That's the one," Tenley said. She spooned in more sugar and stirred. "I heard it was a pretty bad breakup."

"Yeah," Matt agreed with a shudder.

Brenna suspected this was a vast understatement. "What happened?"

"Well, she didn't go all *Fatal Attraction* and boil a bunny or anything," Tenley said. "But Clue did have a restraining order out on her for a while, something about stalking."

"Great," Brenna said. "Maybe I'll start with the one who got cheated on first."

She noticed that neither of them offered to ride shot-gun. That couldn't be good.

"I did stop by for another reason," Matt said. "I was hoping to treat you two to dinner at the Fife and Drum. Our chef is trying out a new entrée, Ahi tuna steaks with wasabi, and I knew you'd had a rough day and thought you could use a good meal."

Brenna was touched, truly, but she already had a date.

"I can't," she said. "I'm watching Hank for Nate, and I really don't think I want to be late in feeding him his dinner. It might bode ill for my cabin."

"Another time then?" Matt asked.

"No, don't put it off on my account," Brenna said. "Tenley can go. She has no plans."

"Oh, no, I couldn't," she said.

"Yes, you can," Brenna said. "In fact, I insist. Matt, take her to dinner and I'll lock up the shop tonight."

"But . . ."

"No buts," Brenna said. She stood and gathered their mugs. "Be sure to order seconds of the amaretto cheese-cake for me."

Matt stood with a smile. "Well, if that's an order, shall we?"

"Well, okay, I guess," Tenley agreed.

Funny, for someone who sounded so reluctant, she looked pretty happy about this turn of events.

Brenna locked the door behind them with a wave and a smile. She had been hoping to shove them together at some point, as it was obvious they still liked each other, and it was equally obvious that neither of them had any idea what to do about it. She was pleased to help out, even if it meant skipping a free dinner.

She drove home with the windows down, letting in the warm evening air and the musical chirp of the spring peepers, small frogs that inhabited the woods around Morse Point Lake. She was looking forward to seeing Hank. There was a little part of her that wished she were going home to Nate, too. But if she couldn't have the man, she'd happily take the dog.

Hank bounced in circles of canine delight when Brenna pushed open the door of her cabin. He jumped up and licked her chin, her ear, and her nose. She laughed as she wiped off the doggie slobber with her sleeve. Dinner would have to wait. Hank needed some playtime.

She grabbed two of his tennis balls and they headed to the lake. She threw one in a high arch and Hank launched himself off of the bank, landed with a big splash, and dog-paddled out to the ball. He retrieved it with his mouth, and Brenna could swear he was grinning. He climbed ashore and shook out his shaggy mane, making sure to splash her—at least she was pretty sure he'd planned that.

She threw the ball again and watched as he dove for it. The late June evening was cooling and the breeze off of the water felt good on her skin. She glanced up and saw her neighbor Twyla leaving her cabin with a beach towel over her arm.

Twyla skipped across the grass toward Brenna. She said skipping kept her young. She was somewhere in her late fifties or early sixties, although she didn't look it, and Brenna believed her.

Twyla was a sculptor, who worked primarily with metal. Behind her cabin, a field of wind sculptures was growing. With rounded shapes, some looked like big steel flowers that spun when the softest breeze captured their metallic petals. Others looked like long, curving spirals, and wound their way from the ground up into the sky. Brenna liked to go and walk amongst them on windy days and feel the power of nature and steel combined into a beautiful form.

Twyla joined Brenna by the water's edge and handed her the towel. "You're going to need that."

"Thanks." Brenna dabbed at her face and shirt.

"Nate always forgets to bring a towel, too," she said. "But usually he goes fishing afterward and lets Hank air dry."

"I'm not going fishing," Brenna said.

"I figured," Twyla said. She tossed her thick gray braid over her shoulder and brushed a hand over her iridescent green, broomstick skirt. "So, I heard you were the one who found Clue Parker with an axe lodged in his head."

"There was no axe," Brenna spluttered. "And his head was intact. Honestly, how do these rumors get so out of control?"

"But you did find him?" Twyla asked.

"Yes," she admitted. Hank jumped onto the bank and shook himself from head to tail. Brenna took the ball he dropped and threw it as far as she could.

"Are you okay?" Twyla asked. Her eyes were round with concern, and Brenna was grateful.

"I will be," she said. "Better than Clue at any rate."

"It's a bad business," Twyla said. "First the mayor and now this young man. What do you suppose is happening to our sleepy little Morse Point?"

"I wish I could say," Brenna said.

Twyla said nothing but remained silently beside her. She had an inner serenity from her metalwork that Brenna understood. She felt the same way about her paper work. Taking cutouts and a beat-up old piece of furniture and marrying the two into something beautiful made sense to her, as if she could create order out of chaos.

There was no sense to be made out of Clue's murder, however. She could still see him, lying in the bed in a pool of blood, dead. But who had killed him and why?

The sun dipped lower and the breeze blew colder. To Brenna it felt as if the ghost of the recently departed passed through her on the way to his next stop. But maybe she just needed to go get her sweater.

Chapter 7

Brenna did not need any stamps. She had bought the Liberty Bell Forever stamps the last time they'd been offered, and she'd bought a lot of them. Still, she didn't have any packages to mail or bills to post, so buying stamps was the best excuse she could come up with to pay Bonnie Jeffries a visit.

She didn't know what to expect, but the cute little redhead at the counter sure wasn't it. She was allover petite, from her tiny upturned nose to her dainty little feet. She wore her hair in a short cap of strawberry curls, freckles were sprinkled liberally over her skin, and her eyes were the brightest blue, almost as if they were lit from the inside, that Brenna had ever seen.

She loitered by the display of packing materials, waiting while Mr. Portnoy mailed his sister in Illinois a big block of cheese and again while Mrs. Hutchins tried to figure out what was cheaper, first class or priority, on a wedding gift for her sister in Florida. It was a sister that she wasn't particularly fond of, and it was her third wedding, so she ended up mailing it book rate, figuring her sister would probably be divorced again by the time it arrived anyway.

When it was just Bonnie and her in the small office, Brenna approached the counter.

"May I help you?" Bonnie asked.

"Hi, I'm . . ." she began, but Bonnie cut her off and said, "Brenna Miller, who works at Vintage Papers for Tenley Morse, who solved the mayor's murder last April and who found the body of Clue Parker yesterday."

"That's me," Brenna confirmed. Apparently, Bonnie had a little bit of firecracker in her.

"And I'm betting you're here to ask me about my relationship with Clue Parker and try to figure out if I was angry enough at him to want him dead, like every other busybody in town?"

So much for trying to loosen her up with small talk. Bonnie was as direct as a hammer on a thumb.

"Or I could just be here to buy stamps," Brenna said.

"Stamps, right."

She opened a drawer in the desk in front of her. She began sorting her stamps. She laid a few sheets out on the counter for Brenna to look over.

"He slept with my mother," Bonnie said. "He was an immoral tomcat who destroyed anyone who got close to him."

"I'm sorry," Brenna said.

Red splotches bloomed in Bonnie's cheeks, and Brenna couldn't tell if it was from embarrassment or anger.

"It's been three years since I've spoken to either him or my mother. Did he deserve to die? Yeah. Did I do it? I only wish."

"So, you haven't spoken to him?" Brenna asked.

"No," Bonnie said. "And I told Chief Barker the same thing."

"Do you know anyone else who was angry with him?" Brenna asked. She picked up a sheet of the mother and child stamps and studied them. They would make a lovely accent on some of the Italian papers Tenley had bought for the store.

"Any woman he took to bed and then dumped," Bonnie said. "Which is probably what happened with little Miss Moneybags."

Brenna met Bonnie's gaze and asked, "What do you mean?"

Bonnie let out a pent-up sigh. "Simply that if Clue got it in his head that he was going to have her, she didn't stand a chance."

"But she's marrying his best friend," Brenna protested.

Bonnie gave her a look that said she was too dumb to cross the street without parental supervision.

"Jake and Clue have been attached at the hip since first grade. Jake has always looked out for Clue and kept him out of trouble. How do you think Clue felt about losing his wingman to the spoiled princess?"

Brenna was again reminded of the look she'd seen on Clue's face when he looked at Tara on the night of the bachelorette party. He hated her.

"Not happy," Brenna said.

"Yeah," Bonnie agreed. "Clue was a master manipulator, and I'm guessing he maneuvered her into bed, convincing her that he was really the man for her, not Jake. Then when she found out that he did it just to ruin her marriage to Jake, she stabbed him."

"Whoa," Brenna said.

The door opened and Mr. Portnoy rushed in.

"Bonnie, I thought about it, and I want to put tracking on that package to my sister," he said. "I can't have two pounds of cheese going astray."

"Certainly, Mr. Portnoy," Bonnie said and then looked back at Brenna. "Are we finished here?"

"For now," Brenna said. She handed Bonnie the cash for the stamps and put them in her purse. "Have a good day."

"Yeah, right."

Brenna stepped out of the post office into the bright morning light. The air was warm already and promised to be steamy by midday. The post office was on the opposite side of the town green from Vintage Papers, and Brenna could see that Tenley had already turned the Closed sign to Open on the front door. It was time to get to work.

She'd have to track down Clue's other girlfriend, the stalker, later. She had a sinking feeling, though, that the information would be the same. And it made sense. If Clue was a womanizer, why wouldn't he use his prowess on Tara and wreck her marriage to Jake, thus saving his friendship?

Because Jake would never forgive him, she thought. So, he wouldn't be saving his friendship at all but destroying it for good. Why would he do that? Unless he was angry with Jake and feeling abandoned by him and figured he had nothing to lose.

Ugh. Her head was beginning to hurt. Brenna crossed the street and took one of the cobbled walkways that led across the green. She inhaled the scent of the freshly mowed grass and tried to calm her mind. She could hear the tweet and twitter of the songbirds up in the trees, and the flower beds around the gazebo were a profusion of purple, pink, and white petunias.

It was a lovely day. Too bad Clue Parker wasn't here to enjoy it, and if Tara was locked up for his murder, she wouldn't be enjoying it either.

"Did you talk to Bonnie?" Tenley asked as soon as she stepped through the front door.

"Yep," Brenna said. "She thinks Clue wooed Tara to break up the marriage and then when she found out the truth, she stabbed him."

"Grisly," Tenley said.

"Too grisly," Brenna said. "I just don't see it."

"Me either," Tenley agreed. "So, what next?"

"You tell me how dinner went with Matt," Brenna said.

Tenley flushed a deep pink and Brenna clapped her hands.

"It went great, didn't it? Are you going to see him again? Did you kiss him? Come on, dish!"

"He was a perfect gentleman," Tenley said. She sounded annoyed by it. "But he did ask me if I'd like to do it again sometime."

"And you said . . ."

"Yes. I said yes," Tenley said.

"Good girl!" Brenna cheered.

A chime sounded from her purse. She flipped the top of her black backpack purse open and fished around for her cell phone.

"Hello?" she answered.

"So, how much obedience school is Hank going to need when I get back?"

"Hi," Brenna said. She felt her own face grow warm at the sound of Nate's voice. "I'll have you know, I've been working on his table manners and other than his resistance to using a fork, he's doing quite well."

"Oh, really?"

"Yep, the lack of an opposable thumb is a disadvantage, but he's got the napkin on the lap thing down and even asks, well barks, to be excused."

"Next you'll have him doing dishes."

"And if I succeed, you can't have him back."

"Is that Nate?" Tenley asked loud enough to be heard on the phone.

"Tell Tenley I said hi," he said.

"He says hi," Brenna said.

"Don't forget to tell him about the murder," Tenley said, leaning over the table and yelling into the receiver.

"Murder?" Nate asked. "What murder?"

"And that you found the body," Tenley added.

"Brenna, what's going on?" he asked. "What's Tenley talking about?"

"It's been a busy few days here in Morse Point," she said.

"Are you all right?" he asked.

"I'm fine, better than Tara Montgomery in any event," she said. She tried to ignore the fluttery feeling she got at the sound of concern in his voice. Of course he was concerned. She was his tenant. There had been a murder in town. He'd have to be a rock not to be concerned.

"Tara? The girl we saw holding hands with Jake Haywood on the green?" he asked.

Brenna was surprised he remembered, but then she realized not much got by Nate Williams and those piercing gray eyes of his.

"Yes, I found her in bed with Jake's best friend Clue Parker, who was dead, stabbed in the chest. She was holding a knife."

"Whoa," Nate said. "Did Chief Barker take her in?"

"I believe she's been questioned but not officially charged," Brenna said.

"Oh, no," he said.

"What?" she asked.

"You've got that tone of voice again," he said.

"What tone of voice?"

Tenley broke out in a grin as if she knew Brenna was about to get lectured. She turned her back on Tenley to lean against the table and stare at the wall.

"That tone of voice that says you don't think Tara did it and you're going to prove it."

"I don't think you can get all of that out of a tone of voice," she said.

"It's the same voice you used on me when you decided I was innocent and you were going to help me whether I liked it or not."

There was a pause while Brenna considered her words.

"I was right about you," she said.

"You almost got yourself killed," he countered.

She was silent. He was right, but she wasn't about to admit it.

"I'll be home the day after tomorrow," he said. "Promise me you won't do anything until I get back. I'll even help you."

"Where are you?" she asked. She didn't mean to be intrusive: it just slipped out. To her surprise he answered right away, "Connecticut."

"Oh," she said. Now, of course, she had a million more questions, but no idea how to get them out without being rude. Sadly, Nate didn't give her the chance.

"Remember," he said. "You're not to do anything until I get back."

"Uh-huh, I'll give Hank your love," she said, and hung up. She was relieved that she hadn't actually promised and couldn't be held accountable for anything that might come up.

"You're blushing," Tenley said.

"It's just hot in here," Brenna argued.

"It's seventy-four degrees."

"Well, it feels like ninety," Brenna said. "Now where were we?"

"Prepping for your class tonight," Tenley said.

"Right," Brenna said.

She dug into the bottom of the armoire and pulled out a bucket full of two-inch wooden blocks. They were going to make picture puzzles. She took several four-by-six-inch pictures of Hank and put them on the table. She needed six and she had one extra in case of an error. She laid out six blocks and then began cutting the pictures into two-by-six-inch strips.

"Block puzzles," Tenley cried. "I love those."

"Me, too," Brenna agreed. She'd been making these for years and they were always a hit. If this one of Hank turned out well, she might just give it to Nate for his birthday; then again, she wasn't sure when his birthday was. Maybe it could be a Christmas gift.

This picture of Hank featured him with his tongue hanging out while he begged for treats. Then again, maybe she'd keep it. After all, Nate got to keep Hank.

"How do you keep all of them straight?" Tenley asked.

"The key is to finish one picture, then turn the cubes to work on another picture. That way they don't get mixed up and every picture is solvable."

"So, with each side of the cubes being used, it's six puzzles in one," Tenley said.

"Exactly," Brenna said.

"The class will love it."

"I hope so," Brenna said. "It's going to take a couple of weeks to complete. I did tell everyone to bring pictures on thick paper—thin paper won't work. If they don't have enough, we could always use the old greeting cards we've collected."

"I'm going to use my collection of daylily photos," Tenley said. "A different-colored lily for each side, perfect for spring."

"Oh, I like it," Brenna said. "You know, if we made a bunch of them, we could sell them in the store."

"I like the way you're thinking."

They worked quietly for the rest of the afternoon.

Brenna ran home for an early dinner and decided to bring Hank back with her. She hoped Tenley wouldn't mind, but she really felt Hank could use some company.

She brought his favorite chew toy, a squeaky duck, and his bed. As if aware that he was to be on his best behavior, Hank licked Tenley's hand, took his duck, and retired to his bed in front of the window.

The bells jangled on the front door and in trooped Brenna's first students, Marie and Ella Porter. She smiled at the two ladies as they made their way to the refreshment cart.

"Any news?" Ella asked. Her look was sly, and Brenna wondered what she was thinking.

"Meaning?" Brenna asked.

"Are you making any progress asking questions about Clue Parker?" Marie asked as she loaded a plate with cheese and crackers and took a seat at the table.

"What makes you think I'm asking questions about him?"

Ella raised her eyebrows in a smug look. "Elijah Portnoy saw you talking to Bonnie in the post office when he was mailing that big block of cheese to his sister. Everyone knows that Clue broke her heart by sleeping with her mother. If you weren't asking her about Clue what were you doing?"

"Buying stamps," Brenna said.

Marie made a clucking sound. "Of course you were."

Luckily, Sarah Buttercomb from the bakery chose that moment to arrive, bearing a big pink box full of goodies.

The ladies crowded around the refreshment tray while she unloaded macaroons, éclairs, and an assortment of petit fours.

Brenna gave Sarah a one-armed hug. "Have I told you lately how much I love that you're taking my class?"

Sarah laughed and Lillian Page, who had just arrived, teased, "Teacher's pet!"

"Bring me chocolate," Brenna said. "I have enough love for everyone."

The bells on the door jangled again and in walked Margie Haywood, Jake's mother. An unnatural hush fell over the group as if no one knew quite what to say.

"You're just in time, Margie," Brenna said. She was determined to treat her as if nothing was different. "Sarah brought éclairs. I know how much you like those."

Margie smiled her thanks at Brenna. Meanwhile, Tenley loaded a plate for her and helped her to her seat.

"I hope you all remembered to bring in some photos," Brenna said. "If not, I have pictures you can use. But here is what we're going to be working on."

It had taken her all afternoon, and she still had to put the finish on the cubes, but in essence the project was done. She put the pieces on the table and demonstrated how the block puzzles worked. A buzz of interest filled the room, and Brenna was grateful. She knew this was a project her students could use again and again.

They spent the next two hours happily cutting and pasting and snacking their way through the evening. Even Margie managed a small smile or two. The class was just cleaning up after themselves when Ella called from the refreshment table, "Hey, who finished off the macaroons?"

"Not me," Marie said. "I don't like coconut."

"Well, I could have sworn there was a whole plateful here a minute ago and now they're all gone," Ella said. "You know there's no need to go making a pig out of yourself, ladies."

A belch sounded.

Everyone glanced around the room to catch the culprit with the bad manners. Another belch sounded, and this time, Brenna knew it came from the shaggy blond sitting by the window.

"Hank!" she called in her sternest voice. "Did you eat the macaroons?"

He lowered his head and put his paws over his nose.

"Oh, isn't he precious?" Sarah asked.

"No, he is not," Brenna said. "Especially if he throws up all night long. You are in time-out, mister."

He gave her his best sad-eyed look, but Brenna just pointed at the wall and said, "Go."

Hank slunk off of his bed and sat on his haunches, facing the wall.

"How long will he sit like that?" Sarah asked. She looked worried, and Brenna remembered she had three dogs of her own and doted on them.

"Just for a few minutes," Brenna reassured her.

As if he knew there was a sucker in the room, Hank turned his head to gaze at them over his shoulder, looking just pitiful.

"Oh, look how sorry he is," Sarah said.

"Yeah, all of my boys have mastered that look," Lillian said. "He's playing you. Don't fall for it."

Brenna smiled. Lillian might talk tough, but her boys were her life. In fact, Brenna noticed her picture puzzle was all photos of her boys.

"Hank, are you ready to come out of time-out?" Brenna asked. His tail thumped on the ground. "All right, but behave."

He trotted to sit beside her and as he leaned against her, he licked her hand. Brenna couldn't help but scratch his head. She wasn't spoiling him, really.

"He really is a good dog," Margie Haywood said. "Jake should have had a dog like that growing up, maybe then he wouldn't have become friends with—"

Her voice cracked and she ducked her head. Brenna saw several tears stream down her cheeks and she quickly grabbed a tissue out of a nearby box and handed it to her.

"If you'll excuse me," Margie said. She quickly gathered her purse and left the shop without a backward glance.

"Poor thing," Marie said. "This should have been the happiest time of her life, planning her son's wedding, and instead, he might go to jail for murdering his best friend."

"What?" Tenley asked. "But that's ridiculous. Jake Haywood would never hurt anyone and definitely not his best friend, no matter what that friend did to him."

The room was silent. Brenna knew they were all thinking about being in Jake's shoes, about being betrayed by the two people they loved most. Honestly, she thought that could drive anyone to commit murder, even a man as nice as Jake Haywood.

Chapter 8

As the others departed and the Porter sisters lingered, Brenna decided it was a good time to tap in to their collective knowledge about the residents of Morse Point, specifically Clue Parker.

She sidled over to Tenley, who was gathering the dishes off of the refreshment table.

"Do me a favor?" she asked.

"Anything but take the macaroon-barfing dog to my house," she said.

"He's got a stomach made of iron," Brenna assured her. "I think he only barfs healthy food like broccoli or carrots. Anyway, that's not it. What I need you to do is find out everything Marie knows about Clue Parker while I do the same with Ella."

"Separate the dynamic duo? Why?"

"I think we'll get more accurate information that way."

"Ella is the tougher nut," Tenley said.

"I know. Nice of me to let you have Marie, yes?"

"Very," Tenley agreed. "Marie, could you help me in the break room with these dishes?"

"Certainly, dear," Marie said and followed Tenley into the back.

Brenna sat across the table from Ella. Together they cleared the tabletop of photo scraps and sticky glue spots.

"So, Ella, did you know the Parker family very well?"

Ella glanced up from her sponge and narrowed her gaze at Brenna.

"As well as anyone and better than most, I expect," she said.

"Good family?"

"Humph," Ella snorted. "If you consider a father who pickled himself in a whiskey bottle every day and a mother who lifted her skirt for anything in pants good."

"So, Clue had a rough childhood?"

"In every way except for his friendship with Jake," she said. "Jake protected him as much as he could, brought him home every day and made sure he was fed. Clue practically grew up at the Haywoods'. They took him in as if he was their own, although I know Margie didn't approve of his wild womanizing ways."

Brenna was silent while Ella gathered her thoughts.

"Clue would have turned out much worse if it weren't for Jake. In fact, he probably wouldn't have survived his teen years at all. But Jake kept him out of trouble and got him a job at the paper factory over in Milstead. He's been there since he graduated high school, which he never would have managed if Jake hadn't dragged him to school with him."

"The Milstead Paper Factory?" Brenna said. "I thought he worked at the Brass Rail as a bouncer."

"He did both," Ella said. "He had to pay for all those fancy motorbikes of his somehow."

"I suppose," Brenna said.

"Thanks for your help, Marie," Tenley said as they re-entered the shop.

"My pleasure," Marie said. "Well, Sis, are you ready to go?"

Ella glanced at Brenna and nodded. "Yes, I think so."

"Good night, ladies," Tenley said as she locked the door behind them.

She switched off the main lights and she and Brenna went to the break room to gather their things before slipping out the back.

"Come on, Hank," Brenna called.

He wagged his way across the room, happy to be in her good graces again. Brenna clipped on his leash and they stepped out into the warm evening air. Tenley locked the door after them.

"So, what did you get?" Tenley asked as they made their way up the alley.

"The only thing new is that he worked at the paper mill over in Milstead."

"I got that, too," Tenley said. "And according to Marie, they had a falling out over a girl a few years back."

Brenna stopped short. "Tell."

"You remember the girl we talked about, the one who used to ride around the town green on the back of Clue's bike but left to go be a chef in Boston?"

"Lisa Sutton," Brenna said.

"That's right. Well, apparently, she left because she was in love with Jake," Tenley said. "She threw herself at him and he turned her down because of his friendship with Clue. Clue didn't quite see it that way and blamed Jake for driving her away. She is the only woman known to have rejected Clue, and he didn't take it well."

"How did you get all this and I didn't?"

"You know Marie has a weakness for love stories, especially of the unrequited kind."

"True. Ella is more hard facts," Brenna agreed. "You don't think Clue seduced Tara to get even, do you?"

Tenley shrugged. "People do crazy things when it comes to love."

They reached their cars and Brenna pressed her key fob until her Jeep unlocked with a click. She opened the passenger side for Hank to jump up into and then walked around the front.

"So, I was thinking I'd drive out to the paper mill tomorrow," she said.

"Great. I've been planning to go and check them out for the shop," Tenley said. "Here at eight o'clock?"

"See you then," Brenna agreed with a grin.

She would have argued, but Tenley had that stubborn Morse set to her chin, and Brenna knew there would be no shaking her. Besides, with Tenley along, she really could be checking out the mill for the shop, so if it happened to get back to Chief Barker that she was there, it was as innocent as buttercups and daisies.

The white clouds being exhaled from the mill's smokestacks made the factory easy to spot even against the morning's overcast sky.

Tenley sipped her latte to-go from Stan's Diner while Brenna drove her Jeep down the winding road that led to the mill.

Nestled on the banks of the Milstead River, the mill looked like a complicated puzzle of large rectangular buildings, concrete slabs, steel silos, and pipes. Up close, it was even more intimidating.

Brenna pulled up to the security gate and rolled down her window. A man with a clipboard looked at them and they both turned the wattage of their smiles up to blinding.

"Can I help you?" he asked. Brenna wasn't sure, but he

looked to be in his midforties, with thinning hair and the requisite middle-aged paunch, which he was valiantly trying to suck in behind his waistband.

"Hi, we're from Vintage Papers over in Morse Point," Brenna said. "We're here to visit your showroom."

"Go right ahead." He gestured toward the large lot. "Public parking is on the left."

"Thank you," they both said.

As Brenna drove away, she watched in the rearview mirror as he sagged back into his post. She wished she could have asked him about Clue, but probably starting with security was not the best plan.

She parked in the lot marked Visitors and she and Tenley climbed out. They had worked on their cover story over their lattes earlier, and she was going to let Tenley, as the owner of Vintage Papers, take the lead.

Basically, Tenley was looking to get into the office supply business and could she work a deal with them since they were both local *yada yada yada*. Brenna was just hoping to poke around and find a gossipy salesperson or two who could tell her what Clue was like on the job.

They walked into the main lobby, which was also their storefront, to find it full, hip to hip, with people wearing hard hats. A woman in professional attire, a navy blue business skirt with a white ruffled blouse, and navy heels, waved to them over the crowd.

"Are you here for the tour?"

Brenna and Tenley exchanged a look.

"Yes," they said together.

"Great," the woman chirped. She had a hard hat cradled under her arm and she plunked it on her short brunette head as she said, "I'm Sally. Name tags and hard hats are on the counter. Suit up and follow us."

With that she pushed through the double doors into a long hallway. Tenley took two hard hats, while Brenna wrote their names on the self-adhesive "Hello, my name is . . ." badges.

Tenley glanced at hers. "Patty?" Then she looked at Brenna's. "And Selma? Lovely."

"Don't blow our cover, Patty," Brenna chided.

Tenley rolled her eyes.

They trailed behind the group, listening to Sally talk about the history of the paper mill as they went. The group stopped beside a large floor to ceiling poster of an artist's rendering of the first mill.

"Built in 1848, the mill is one of the oldest in the country," Sally began. "There were thirty-nine employees at the time it opened producing two thousand pounds of paper per day."

The group worked their way past several more pictures and Sally spoke of the impact of the Civil and World wars on the paper industry.

Brenna had to admit, despite her interest in finding out about Clue, it was a fascinating bit of American history.

Glass display cases lined the walls, showing examples of some of the products the paper made by the mill was used for over the years; McGuffy Readers for schoolchildren and the old *Morse Point Courier*. Ed Johnson, the current editor of the *Courier*, had caused Brenna quite a bit of grief a few months back, but he had mellowed considerably after she rescued him from being the next victim of a murderer.

Brenna and Tenley exchanged a look. Brenna was sure she was thinking about Ed, too, before they followed the group down the hall.

"Next we have our executive offices," Sally said. "This is where the day-to-day operations are overseen."

They entered a room sectioned off by cubicles. Brenna slowed to look at one that had a row of troll dolls with bright-colored hair looking down on the occupant.

A matronly woman with stylish gray hair wearing reading glasses looked up at her and winked. "Good-luck charms. They ward off evil bosses."

Brenna laughed. Tenley lowered an eyebrow at her and said, "Don't get any ideas."

Phones were ringing and the sound of fingers clacking against computer keyboards filled the room against a backdrop of people chatter. It certainly seemed like a happy, prosperous place.

Sally led them across the room into a large break room. Coffee and doughnuts and a bowl of fresh fruit had been put out on a far table. Brenna felt her stomach rumble, but she tried to ignore it. A set of windows looked over the woods beyond the plant, and on the other side of the room another set of windows looked down on the plant below.

Sally paused by the windows overlooking the plant. "For the safety of everyone on the tour, we'll be overseeing the plant operations from a steel catwalk. It is mostly enclosed, but there are sections that are open. If anyone here has a fear of heights, you might want to wait as we'll be ending the twenty-minute tour right here in this room."

"How high is the catwalk?" a woman asked. She was tall and thin, wearing a beige business suit and looking ill at ease.

"Thirty feet," Sally said.

"I think I'm going to wait here," the woman said.

"Oh, come on, Jane, you can do it," another woman, shorter and huskier, encouraged her. There was something in her tone, however, that made Brenna think the short one was enjoying the other woman's unease.

"Tell you what, Jane, I'll wait with you," a man said. "We can eat all of the doughnuts before they get back."

"Oh, you don't have to do that," Jane protested.

"Really, Kyle, she's not a child, she can wait by herself," the other woman said, looking unpleasant.

"True, but I've been on this tour before and this will give us a chance to go over the prospectus for next quarter," he said.

"Shall we then?" Sally asked with a pointed glance at her watch.

"Drama in the office," Tenley whispered to Brenna.

"Indeed."

They followed Sally through a set of double doors and down the narrow catwalk. Parts of it were enclosed and they looked through the glass to the operation below. Brenna had to admit it was a fascinating process to see wood chips transformed into pulp and pressed into paper.

They learned that hardwood trees such as oaks and maples have wood with very short fibers. Paper made from these trees is weaker than that made from softwoods, but the surface is smoother, making it better for writing and printing.

Conversely, softwood trees, such as pine and spruce, have wood with long fibers, which make a much stronger paper that is better used for cardboard boxes and other packaging materials.

The mill was also a depository for recycled paper, which they re-pulped to be pressed and used again.

While the group paused to study a display board about the recycling process at the plant, Brenna took the opportunity to chat with Sally. Since they were above the floor where Clue had worked, and there was no direct access to the plant, she knew she wasn't going to have an opportunity to talk to anyone down there.

"Sally, I noticed a copy of the *Morse Point Courier* in the display case at the beginning of the tour."

"Oh, yes, we've supplied their paper for almost a century," she said, nodding.

"I live in Morse Point," Brenna said.

"Lovely town, very quaint," Sally said. She smiled and

nodded again and Brenna was reminded of a bobblehead doll.

"It is a small town," Brenna said. "The residents are very close."

Sally stopped nodding and looked cautious, as if she wasn't quite sure what to say when it wasn't scripted. Brenna suspected she knew what was coming so she forged ahead before Sally could get away. "Did you know Clue Parker very well?"

Sally looked from left to right, as if hoping for a rescue.

"I only ask because I know he worked here," Brenna said.

"I knew of him," Sally said. "I'm in charge of community outreach, so I didn't have much contact with workers from the floor."

"Was he well liked?" Brenna asked.

Sally's hand fluttered around her throat. Brenna did not need a degree in psychology to know she was hiding something. Something big. It hit Brenna with a blast of awareness.

"Did you have a relationship with him?" she asked.

"I don't know what you're talking about," Sally snapped. Her hands dropped and fisted at her sides. She tossed her head, making her hair fall back from her face. "I am happily married."

"My mistake," Brenna said. "It's just that Clue had such a reputation . . ."

"Listen, Ms. Selma, I really don't know anything about Mr. Parker," she said. "Now if you'll just rejoin the group."

Brenna could tell she was upset, and she felt badly to have caused it, but still she knew Sally was hiding something.

"I'm sorry, I didn't mean to upset you," she said.

Sally gave her a curt nod but didn't make eye contact.

Brenna rejoined Tenley.

"Get anything?" Tenley asked.

"All I can say is *whoa*."

"Tell."

"Later."

"All right everyone." Sally clapped her hands. "It's time to head back to the main room. If you'll follow me."

They moved at a clip back to the conference room with the refreshments. Brenna wondered if she could chat up the lady with the troll dolls when they got back.

"I'm going to see what I can get out of the sales guys when we get back," Tenley said. "And you?"

"Office staff," Brenna said. "I want to know more about Sally the tour guide."

"Ooh," Tenley said with raised eyebrows.

They entered the break room, where Sally, looking more composed, fielded some questions. Brenna and Tenley slunk out the door back to the main room, where Tenley was greeted by a salesman, who had the look of a shark, while Brenna made her way toward the troll-collecting lady in the cubicle. She was halfway there when a hand grabbed her elbow, stopping her.

Chapter 9

"Brenna Miller, or are you going by Selma now?" Brenna turned and found herself face-to-face with Dom Cappicola. He smiled and said, "We have to stop meeting like this."

She should have felt the change in the energy of the room. Dom exuded raw power like some men wore too much cologne. Until you were used to it, it overpowered.

Luckily, she knew Dom well enough to know it wasn't his fault. It was in his genes to make the people around him nervous. He was a Cappicola, one of New England's premier mob families, and even though he was going legit, he had generations of bad boy in him that were impossible to ignore.

"Hi," she said. "Why am I not more surprised to see you?"

He shrugged. "What can I say? I'm the bad penny that keeps turning up."

Brenna could feel the eyes of every woman in the room

on them; some were curious. others were envious. Either way, it didn't suit her purposes to be so noticed.

"Are you here for the tour, too?" she asked, trying to keep it casual.

"No, I'm here to go over the quarterly report with the manager," he said. "I own this place."

"You are kidding me," she said.

"I never kid about business." He grinned. "Come on, I'll show you my office."

Brenna followed him to the side of the room that housed the offices with windows. Dom's was in the corner, with the best view of the river splitting the hills beyond.

"Can I get you anything?" he offered.

"No, thank you," she said.

Two leather wing chairs were placed in front of the window and Brenna went to stand by those while he stopped at his desk and picked up his phone.

"Rich, something unexpected has come up," he said. His eyes twinkled at Brenna. "Let's push back our meeting another twenty minutes."

He hung up and joined Brenna by the chairs. When they were both seated, he said, "Okay, you didn't know I owned this place, so it obviously wasn't me that brought you here, so what did? And what's with the name tag, Selma?"

"Paper," she offered. "Tenley, or rather Patty, is meeting with one of your salesmen right now."

"Patty and Selma from *The Simpsons*? Funny. But why are aliases necessary?"

"We didn't want to be pestered by salespeople if we decided to go another way," she said.

"But we make primarily office paper," he said. "Vintage Papers is all that froufrou specialty stuff."

"We're diversifying," she said.

He pursed his lips and studied her. "Are you aware that when you lie, your eyes become greener?"

"They do not," she said. He raised his brows, and she said, "I'm not lying—do they really?"

"No, but they may as well," he said. "You're a terrible liar."

"It's not a complete lie," Brenna protested. "Tenley is meeting with one of your salesmen."

"But . . ."

"But she's trying to get information about one of your employees," she said.

"Just like you were about to go badger my office staff," he guessed.

"*Badger* is such an ugly word," she said.

"Talk to me, bright eyes," he said. "Maybe I can help."

"All right, but I don't want a lecture," she said.

He nodded in agreement.

"We're here about Clue Parker," she said.

"The mill worker who was murdered?" he asked. "I know he was from Morse Point, but what's the connection to you? You weren't dating him, were you?"

He looked annoyed. Brenna gave him a flat stare, and he had the grace to look embarrassed.

"Sorry, but the guy certainly blew through the ladies around here."

"Around everywhere, apparently," she said. "You remember the night we saw you at the Willow House?"

He looked her up and down and Brenna knew he was remembering the dress she wore that night. "Oh, yeah."

She ignored the flush that heated her face. "Well, that was the bachelorette party for the woman he was found in bed with the next day. I'm the one who found him."

Dom's eyes went wide and he sat forward in his seat. His look was worried when he studied her face. "Brenna, I'm so sorry. That must have been—are you okay?"

His concern made her feel more vulnerable than she had in days, and she had to swallow past the knot in her throat before she could speak.

"The thing is Tara, the bride, is the main suspect, and I just don't think she did it," she said.

"Oh, no," he said with a shake of his head. "Please tell me you are not getting involved in another murder case."

"I'm not getting involved in another murder case," she said. "I'm just trying to help out a friend by looking for another viable suspect."

Dom leaned back in his chair and blew out a pent-up breath. "So, you're here to ask questions about Clue and see if someone else had a motive to murder him?"

"That sounds about right," she said. "So, how well did you know him?"

"If I don't help you, you're just going to forge ahead on your own, aren't you?" he asked.

"I refuse to answer on the grounds that I'll incriminate myself," she said.

He sighed. "I knew he worked in the plant, and I knew he had a rep with the ladies, but personally, no, I didn't know him."

"Got any idea who might?" she asked.

"Oh, no, you don't," he said. "You are not going to poke around the mill, asking questions. What if the murderer works here and you get them all riled up?"

"Then I'll have a new suspect," she said.

"Or get yourself killed," he snapped.

He lowered an eyebrow and considered her. Then a slow smile spread across his face. "Seven o'clock. Tonight. I'll pick you up."

"Are you asking me or telling me?"

"I'll ask questions today and tell you what I find out over dinner," he said.

"What if I want to ask the questions?" she asked.

"Deal or no deal," he said.

It was a deal, but she didn't say that right away. Instead, she mirrored his look and studied him. His dark hair was short and combed back from his face. His features were square and hard as if he'd seen more of the world than the usual man in an Armani suit.

This was his business and these people worked for him. She had a feeling he would get much more information from them than she would.

Finally, she gave him a slow nod and said, "Deal."

Brenna met Tenley in front of the building. They walked to Brenna's Jeep at the back of the lot.

"So, what did you get?" she asked Tenley.

Tenley took a deep breath and said, "Well, the salesman didn't know him as well as I would have liked, but he did know his reputation. Apparently, he was working his way through the female staff here at the plant, including a torrid affair with our tour guide Sally, who happens to be married, and while there had been no formal complaints to HR, they were keeping an eye on him. How about you? What did you get?"

"A date with a mobster," Brenna said.

Tenley stumbled over her feet and stopped to stare at Brenna.

"Guess who owns Milstead Paper Mill?"

"Dom?"

"Ding! Give the lady the big stuffed giraffe," Brenna said in her best carnival barker's voice. "He's going to nose around for us and then tell me what he finds out over dinner tonight."

"So, you have an actual date?"

"Yep." Brenna unlocked the Jeep and they climbed in.

"But what about Nate?"

"What about him?"

"I sort of thought the two of you . . ."

Brenna steered the car back through the gate, waving to the guard, and down the winding road back to Morse Point.

"As far as I can tell, Nate views me as a tenant and a friend—oh, and a dog sitter," she said.

"Nothing more?"

"No," Brenna said. She ignored the pang she felt at this harsh truth. It was better to be brutally honest than to hope for things that were improbable at best.

"How long has it been since you've had a date?" Tenley asked.

Brenna had to think about it. Her boyfriend James had broken up with her the last year she'd lived in Boston and that was a year and a half ago.

"Two years since James," she said. "Seven if you count anyone but him."

Tenley studied her from head to toe. "Step on it. We have work to do."

Brenna had planned to work in the shop all day and prep for her date after. Tenley had other ideas.

As soon as they parked in front of Vintage Papers, Tenley took Brenna by the hand and dragged her down the sidewalk to Ruby Wolcott's salon Totally Polished.

"Tenley, where are you going? We need to open the shop," Brenna said.

"Detour," Tenley said as she opened the salon door and pushed Brenna inside. "Ruby, we have an emergency!"

Ruby was standing behind the reception desk with her beehive of platinum hair up in a full twist. Her hairdresser's smock was a leopard print with magenta piping and she wore magenta heels to match.

Her drawn-on eyebrows moved up as she took in the sight of them.

"What sort of an emergency?" she asked. "Gum in your hair? Hangnail? What?"

"It's worse," Tenley said.

Two ladies under hair dryers poked their heads out to see what was happening. Ruby's other hairdresser, Mae, paused while clipping the gray head sitting in her chair to hear what was being said.

"How much worse?" Ruby asked.

Tenley pushed Brenna forward. "First date in over two years."

A gasp reverberated around the salon.

"Kelsey," Ruby barked at the young woman sweeping up hair. "Clear the rest of my morning appointments."

"I really don't think this is necessary," Brenna began, but Ruby grabbed her hand and studied her cuticles, "Good God, woman, when was the last time you had a mani? These ragged things looked like you walked on them to get here."

"Have a lovely morning," Tenley said to Brenna as she dashed out the door with a wave.

"I'll get you for this," Brenna growled.

"No, you owe me for this," Tenley corrected her as the door shut behind her, sealing Brenna's fate.

Three hours later, having been thoroughly clipped, snipped, waxed, fluffed, and folded, Brenna left Totally Polished.

She had Pouty Pink nail polish on her fingers and her toes. Her wavy auburn hair had been smoothed and draped down her back with nary a split end in sight. Her eyebrows had been shaped into seductive arches and her makeup made her skin as flawless as cream.

She barely recognized her reflection in the windows of Vintage Papers, and judging by the greet-the-customer smile Tenley gave her when she walked in, she didn't recognize her either.

"Wow!" Tenley said. She jumped up from her seat at

the worktable and circled Brenna. "You looked great the other night, but this is all new levels. Dom is going to have a heart attack."

"Fabulous," Brenna said. "Because I need another dead body in my life."

"What are you wearing?" Tenley asked.

"I'm not sure," Brenna said. "I'm thinking my favorite little black dress."

"The Maggy London striped mesh?"

Brenna nodded.

"He's done for," Tenley said with a shake of her head.

Brenna rolled her eyes. "What's been going on here?"

"The invitations to Larry Goldbaum's bar mitzvah came in, and they look great. I think his mother will be pleased. I sold two of your decoupage cigar boxes."

"Nice," Brenna said.

"And the Porter twins came in demanding to know who your date is."

"How did they find out? I swear they are their own information superhighway," Brenna said as she took a seat at the table. She wanted to work on Betty Cartwright's cedar hope chest, but she glanced at her fingertips and decided it could wait until tomorrow. After all, she should get at least one day's wear out of her manicure before she wrecked it.

"I did use my lengthy stay at the salon to ask about Julie Harper," she said.

"Clue's girlfriend turned stalker?" Tenley sat across from her. "Do tell."

"Ruby said she hasn't been in since Clue's death," Brenna said. "She spends all day in her bathrobe, eating junk food and staring at his picture."

"Do they think she might be the killer?"

"I couldn't really ask her that directly," Brenna said. "I

got the feeling, from the way they kept changing the subject, that they are protective of her, and Ruby was holding a very sharp pair of scissors at the time."

"Wise decision," Tenley agreed.

"I thought so," Brenna said. "I think I'll try to stop and see her tomorrow, however."

"Under what pretense?"

"I don't know. I'm still working that out," she said. "I'm too old to be selling Girl Scout cookies, aren't I?"

"A bit. Listen, why don't you go get ready for your date? We're closing in a few hours—I'm sure I can handle it alone."

"Maybe I will," Brenna said. "That way I can spend some time with Hank before I go out."

"Have fun tonight," Tenley called after her with a wave.

"I'm just gathering information about Clue," Brenna said as she stood and slung her purse over her shoulder.

"I know, but have fun anyway."

"Yeah, yeah."

"And I expect a full report in the morning!" Tenley shouted after her.

Brenna gave her a noncommittal nod and strode to her Jeep. She didn't feel nervous about having dinner with Dom, but there was an undeniable spring in her step and it was a good thing, too. The Porter sisters had just rounded the corner and spotted her. As they sped up their pace, Brenna turned the key and hit the gas. With a cheery wave, she zipped by them and headed home.

"Do not look at me like that," she said.

Hank ignored her command and gave her his best neglected dog woe-is-me face.

"I do not feel guilty for having a date, and you can't make me," Brenna said.

Hank responded with a low whimper.

"We took an hour-long hike, played Frisbee, and you had a lovely dinner," Brenna said. "So don't waste your whining on me."

She stood back from her full-length mirror and checked her image. Her Maggy London ended just above her knees and was created from long, thick stripes of mesh over beige alternating with black satin stripes, having a peekaboo effect of her body beneath. She wore her Weitzman black pumps and carried a matching clutch. She'd kept her hair down and accessorized with the one-carat diamond studs her parents had given her for her college graduation. The effect was flirty but sophisticated and she was pretty sure Dom would approve. Obviously, Hank did not.

There was a knock at the door and Hank erupted into an explosion of barking. Brenna glanced at the clock. Dom was twenty minutes early. Good thing she was ready.

Her heels clacked against the wooden floor as she crossed the living room. Hank was whining at the door and Brenna hoped that Dom liked dogs.

She grabbed Hank's collar and swung the door wide.

"Hi," she said with a smile, but the man standing in the doorway was not who she expected, and she let go of Hank with a jolt of surprise.

Chapter 10

Nate's gray eyes went wide as he took in her appearance, and he neglected to brace himself when Hank launched himself.

"Oh, no!" Brenna cried out as both man and dog went down in a heap. "Sorry."

Hank straddled Nate and licked his face while Nate tried to look around his yellow head at Brenna.

"Okay, boy, okay," Nate said, scratching Hank's ears. "I love you, too."

He rolled out from under Hank, and grabbing a tennis ball off of the porch floor, he threw it overhand out into the yard. Hank took off after it in a spasm of glee.

Nate turned back to Brenna and his gazed raked her from head to toe. "You didn't mention that your dinners with Hank were formal occasions. I can see why you needed to teach him some table manners."

"Actually, I was just getting ready for a date," she said. She felt her face flame hot, which was ridiculous, because

Nate was just her landlord and a friend. Why would he care if she had a date?

"Uh-huh," he said. He followed her into her cabin, although she hadn't invited him, and stood in the center of the living room with his arms crossed over his chest, while she went to retrieve her purse from the bedroom.

"I thought you were coming back tomorrow," she said.

"That was the original plan." His frown deepened when she paused to spritz on some perfume.

He ran a hand through his wavy brown hair, a mannerism Brenna had come to know as a sign of exasperation. He was wearing a charcoal T-shirt with a Yankees logo on it, tucked into well-worn jeans. He looked good, better than she remembered, although it had only been a few days since she'd seen him, and she felt her stupid crush for him rear its annoying head.

"What did you do to your hair?" he asked. He didn't sound pleased.

"Tenley badgered me into visiting Totally Polished and Ruby straightened it," she said. "Does it look bad?"

"No," he said reluctantly. "I just like it the way you usually wear it, all loose and curly."

"Oh." She tried not to feel offended and decided to switch the subject. "So, what was it that brought you home early?"

"You."

"Me?" she asked. She felt her pulse pick up at the thought that he'd come home for her.

"I got a call from Chief Barker. He seems to think you might be butting into the investigation of Clue Parker's murder and wanted me to talk to you," he said.

Her spurt of hope popped like a soap bubble.

"I am not butting in," she protested. She opened her clutch and checked that she had her wallet, keys, and lipstick.

"Really? Then what were you doing at the Milstead Paper Mill this morning?"

"Saying yes to a date with me," a voice answered from the door.

Brenna turned to see Dom Cappicola silhouetted in the doorway.

He was wearing a black Prada suit with a black dress shirt and tie. With his dark hair and eyes, he looked nothing short of dangerous. With a sideways glance, Brenna could almost see Nate's hackles rise.

"Nate, you remember Dom?" she said.

"Cappicola," Nate said and extended his hand.

"Williams." Dom clasped his hand.

Their handshake seemed cordial, but there was a current of hostility pulsing between the two men that was palpable.

Mercifully, Hank chose that moment to come bounding • into the cabin with his ball in his mouth. Dom stepped in front of Brenna as if to protect her, but it wasn't necessary. Hank dropped his ball and sniffed Dom's shoes.

"This is Hank," she said to Dom. "I've been dog sitting him for Nate. He's friendly."

"Oh," Dom said. He smiled at Brenna and Nate as if it all made sense now. He bent down and held out his hand for Hank to sniff. When Hank wagged, he reached over and scratched his ears.

"Hank's bowls and things are all in the kitchen," Brenna said. "Let me get them for you."

"I can do it," Nate said. "You two go ahead. I'll lock up when we leave."

"Are you sure?"

"Absolutely," Nate said. "Thanks for watching him while I was away."

"It was fun," she said. "He's a great dog. It'll be quiet without him around."

"You'll just have to find someone else to hang around in his place," Dom said as he straightened up and looped an arm around her waist.

Nate frowned at him, and Brenna wondered if it was Dom's family connections that Nate disliked or something else.

Dom glanced at his watch. "We'd better go. We have reservations."

"Good night, Nate," Brenna said. She stooped to scratch Hank's head and said, "See you, roomie."

"Have fun," Nate called after them, and Brenna wondered if he was being sarcastic or if that was just wishful thinking on her part.

Dom helped her pick her way across the grassy lawn to his car in the communal parking lot. It was a black Volvo wagon and Brenna looked at him in surprise.

"What?" he asked with a laugh. "You expected a Ferrari or an Escalade? Volvos have a very high safety rating, you know."

"It's just that every time I think I know you, you surprise me," she said.

"Is that a good thing?"

She let him help her into the passenger's seat.

"Yes," she said. She saw him smile as he walked around the car.

He started up the engine, and Brenna glanced back to see Nate, standing on her porch watching them. She felt a sudden longing to stay here and be with him, but she shook it off. He had certainly never alluded to anything more than friendship between them and she didn't want to damage the friendship they already had by letting her feelings get out of hand. Besides, she knew she'd be talking to him soon, as she had a feeling she hadn't heard the last of his conversation with Chief Barker.

Dom took Route 20 out of Morse Point, which was a

relief because she knew it would be all over town if they were seen together. Not that it was a bad thing to be seen with Dom, but she really didn't want to be the focal point of gossip just now.

They didn't speak but let John Legend pour out of the car speakers in a soothing wash of sound. It was several songs later before Dom took an exit that led them down an old postal route. They wound through the woods for a stretch until they came to an old covered bridge.

A rough, dirt parking lot surrounded the bridge and Dom pulled into an available spot. He climbed out and circled the car to get her.

"Have you been here before?" he asked.

"Never," she said.

"You have to walk across the covered bridge to get to the restaurant beyond," he said. "But the food is worth it."

"I think the bridge is worth it," Brenna said. Her love for all things old made her pause to study the red bridge, perched over the shallow rushing river below.

It was lit on each side by spotlights, and moths danced in the warm June air as they flirted with the light.

Dom took Brenna's arm and led her across the uneven wooden boards. They stopped halfway across at one of the small square windows to gaze at the river below.

"It's a beautiful spot," she said.

"I used to think so," he said.

"You don't anymore?"

"Let's just say that next to you, it pales in comparison," he said.

Brenna burst out laughing and he grinned.

"What? Over the top?"

"A little," she said. "But I like it."

He tucked her hand around his elbow and they left the bridge to follow the path to the old Victorian farmhouse, known as the Thistle Inn, beyond.

The inn's restaurant was one of the finest in the area, and although Brenna had heard of it, she'd never eaten there before. She and Dom were led to a table, by a tall floor to ceiling window, which was draped in a thick linen cloth with a white pillar candle circled by a wreath of white roses interspersed with red berries.

It reminded her of the wedding bouquet Tara had been so ecstatic about and from which they were going to design her wedding favors. Brenna frowned. It seemed wrong to be enjoying herself while Tara's life was such a train wreck.

Dom pulled out her chair, and as if she had conjured her by thinking of her, Brenna glanced up to see Tara enter the dining room, flanked by her parents.

She froze halfway into her seat and Dom followed her gaze. "Oh, the bride."

For a split second, Brenna considered pretending she hadn't seen them. A lifetime of good manners prevailed, however, and she dropped her clutch in her chair.

"I should go say hello," she said.

"I'll come with you," he said.

"Oh, no, that's all right," she protested.

He raised an eyebrow at her and took her elbow.

The hostess had seated the Montgomerys at a table by a window across the room. Brenna couldn't help thinking that this was another fine mess she'd gotten herself into as they wound their way through the tables.

In a nutshell, the Montgomerys knew her parents, and she was having dinner with a mobster, reformed, but still, not on her parents' short list of desirable people with whom she should be associating. If word got back to her parents, she was going to have a lot of explaining to do—a situation definitely to be avoided.

She could only hope that Tiffany was so consumed with her daughter's plight that she wouldn't mention seeing Brenna to anyone.

"Hello, Tara," Brenna said as they approached the table. "Mr. and Mrs. Montgomery."

The three of them looked up as one, and Brenna could see the ravages of the past few days on their faces. Tara was sickly pale and her eyes were swollen and red-rimmed as if she'd been crying as soon as she rehydrated her tear ducts. Tiffany was more put together but her face looked tense, and no amount of foundation could hide the sleepless circles under her eyes. Tyler looked strained, his jaw clenched tight, as if he were chewing on a particularly grisly piece of meat.

"Brenna!" Tara jumped up from her seat and threw herself into her arms. "It's so good to see you. Jake won't talk to me and Chief Barker keeps asking me questions, but I don't know anything. I swear I can't remember what happened that night."

A dry sob wracked her body and Brenna hushed her and patted her back. She couldn't help but feel protective of this young woman for all that she was going through.

"Tara," Tiffany said as she rose to stand beside them. "Let's not have a scene."

Tara peeled herself off of Brenna and gave herself a gentle shake. "Of course, I'm sorry," she said. "It's just so good to see a friendly face."

"It's good to see you, too," Brenna said, and meant it.

Tyler stood and extended his hand to Dom. "Tyler Montgomery."

Dom clasped his hand. "Dom Cappicola."

Tiffany and Tyler exchanged a quick look, but not quick enough. Brenna could tell from the widening of Tiffany's eyes that they recognized Dom's family name. Now they were probably thanking their lucky stars that their daughter was only facing a murder rap and not dating a mobster. Brenna wanted to protest that Dom was making the family business legit, but that would be socially awkward at best.

"You look gorgeous," Tara gushed. "Is that a Maggy London?"

"Yes, it's my favorite little black dress," Brenna said.

"Every girl has to have one," Tiffany said.

"Or fifteen, I swear they swap them out like putters," Dom said in an aside to Tyler, who looked momentarily nonplussed and then broke the tension by laughing.

"Do you golf, Dom?" he asked.

"My handicap is in the mid- to low seventies," he said.

Tyler leaned back on his heels and raised his eyebrows. "We should play a round."

"Tyler!" Tiffany protested.

"When things—calm down, of course," he said.

"Of course," Dom agreed with a small smile.

"We'll let you get back to your dinner," Brenna said. "Tara, feel free to call me anytime."

"I will," Tara said, looking tearily grateful.

Dom led Brenna back to their table, and as they resumed their seats, she asked, "Do you really golf?"

"Not a stroke," he said. "But I didn't want them to judge you for dating a mobster's son. And that man's heart lies on the rolling greens of St. Andrews."

"How did you know?" she asked.

"Educated guess. They reek of old money, and I could see his golf tan around his collar."

"You're good," Brenna said. "What are you going to do if he calls you for a game?"

"Feign an injury," he said. "A groin pull, no one ever asks you about those, they don't want to know."

Brenna laughed out loud. The man had charm, she had to give him that.

As if by unspoken agreement, they kept their conversation neutral during dinner, keeping it to favorite vacation spots, movies, and books. It was while they lingered over their coffee, and after the Montgomerys left, that Brenna finally asked the questions that were bubbling up inside of her.

"So, did you find out anything about Clue?"

"First, I have a question for you," he said.

"All right." She stirred a dribble of milk from the small white pitcher into her coffee.

"Are you here just because you want to know what I found out at the mill?"

"No," she said, meeting his gaze. "I'm here because I want to be."

"At the risk of overstepping my bounds, I have to ask, is there something between you and your landlord?"

"Friendship," Brenna said.

She glanced quickly back down at her coffee. She didn't really want to admit that she had an unrequited crush on Nate, but Dom deserved the truth, no matter how embarrassing it was for her.

"I like him—a lot," she said. "But he doesn't return those feelings. Ugh, that makes me sound like such a loser."

"No, it doesn't," Dom said. He reached across the table and took her hand. "It makes him sound like an idiot."

"He's not, he's just . . ."

"Stone-blind?" Dom suggested. "A eunuch?"

Brenna laughed. Dom's hand was warm around hers.

"Listen, I'm not going to push you," he said. "But I'm not going to disappear either. When you get tired of waiting for Prince Charming to get his head out of his derriere, you let me know. In the meantime, I'd like to take you out again—nothing serious, just friends."

"I'd like that," Brenna said.

"All right, here's what I found out about Clue," Dom said as he released her hand and leaned forward, keeping his voice low. "He was never late, rarely called out sick, and knew how to work every piece of machinery on the floor. The men wanted to be like him and the women wanted him. Period. Until they dated him, at which point they hated him. Apparently, he was going through women like a race car goes through tires."

"Lovely," Brenna said. "How did he keep his job if he was treating his female coworkers so badly?"

"He was smart about it," Dom said. "He kept it all off-site. He never did anything at work that would give personnel a reason to discipline him."

"Do you think one of those women got angry enough to kill him?"

Dom sipped his coffee while he considered her question. "I don't know. It's possible."

"I asked Sally, our tour guide, about him," she said. "She got very upset."

"She's married," Dom said. "I don't think she wants her husband to find out that she had a torrid affair with Clue."

"But surely, the police are investigating anyone who had a relationship with him and her husband will find out."

"It's a pretty long list," Dom said. "She may be hoping to fly under the radar."

"That's good news for Tara then," Brenna said. "That there are others with strong motives."

"You found her in bed with the victim, clutching the murder weapon," Dom said. "She seems like a nice kid, but I hear Ted Bundy was a peach, too. Brenna, are you sure she's innocent?"

"Yes."

"One more question," Dom said. "Why are you so interested in this case? Why do you feel like you have to help this girl? Why not leave it to the police?"

"That was more than one," she said.

Dom smiled. "Humor me."

Brenna sighed. She did not like to revisit the past, but surely, if anyone could understand it would be Dom.

"Do you know why I moved to Morse Point?" she asked.

"It's a pretty town," he offered.

"It is," she agreed. "But I'm a Bostonian by birth and I lived my entire life in the city up until two years ago."

"What happened?" he asked.

"It was late at night," she said. "I was doing inventory at the art gallery where I worked when it was robbed. I tried to get away but the burglars cracked me on the temple and knocked me out. Then they cleaned the place out."

"You could have been killed!" He sounded outraged. "Didn't they have a security guard?"

"No, and believe it or not, it gets worse," she said. "The burglars took all of Jean Depaul's work, which I had been inventorying, and my identity. They started offering the pieces on the black market under my name. The police decided I was the inside man on the robbery, even though I was sporting a nasty concussion, and I was prosecuted."

"You were cleared, though," he said. He gave her an empathetic look, and she knew that with his family history, he completely understood.

"Luckily, in an effort to catch me the police went undercover and caught the couple who had taken my identity. Turned out they were wanted in several countries and had stolen other gallery workers' identities. It didn't get me my job back, however, and my reputation was damaged beyond repair."

"So, you feel a kinship with those who are wrongly accused," he said.

"I would have given anything to have just one person in my corner during that time," she said. "Even a stranger."

Dom met her gaze and gave her a firm nod. "All right

then. I'll keep nosing around the mill and see if I can uncover any more information."

He took out his wallet and put several bills in the leather bill folder. Brenna wondered if she should offer to pay half. It seemed like the liberated thing to do, but she suspected Dom would not appreciate the gesture. Maybe she could take him out one night in return. Surely, that would be all right. She really needed to ask Tenley how all this worked. She was so rusty when it came to dating, she was surprised she didn't creak.

Dom handed the leather bill case to their waitress as she passed. "It's all set. Thank you."

"Have a nice night," the waitress said.

Dom held out her chair, and Brenna rose to stand beside him. He looked her up and down and let out a sigh.

"I need you to promise me something," he said. He placed her hand on his elbow and they weaved their way through the tables and out the door.

"What?" she asked as they crossed the lush lawn.

"That you'll be careful," he said. "You'll notice I know better than to ask you to stop asking questions."

"I did notice." She smiled.

They were halfway across the bridge, and she paused to look out the little window and watch the moonlight dance on the rushing water below.

"Dom, I think this is the beginning of a beautiful friendship," she said.

His smile disappeared and he looked at her with an unmistakable heat in his eyes.

"For now," he agreed. "For now."

Chapter 11

The hot water from the shower beat a staccato rhythm on her back while Brenna rolled a bar of soap between her fingers, building up a thick lather that smelled of lavender.

She needed to go and see Julie Harper. The girl had stalked Clue when he was alive and, according to Ruby, had sunk into a depression since his death.

The only problem was she didn't really have a reason to go and see Julie, other than to be nosey and intrusive. She had looked up the girl's address in the phone book and knew that she lived in an old farmhouse on the outskirts of town. There was no way Brenna could pretend to just be walking by. It was too inaccessible and remote.

Too bad she wasn't still watching Hank, or she could take him for a walk in the woods and just happen to turn up in Julie's yard. That was it!

The best ideas always came in the shower. She did a quickie rinse and shut off the water. She didn't need to be dog sitting Hank. She could just borrow him! Nate would say yes, she was sure of it.

She patted herself dry with a fluffy towel and yanked on a pair of jeans and a T-shirt. She ran a comb through her hair, deciding to let it air dry, which would make it curly, but that couldn't be helped. She was on a mission.

She raced down the path that led to Nate's cabin. She knocked three times on the door, and sure enough Hank went into a barking frenzy. Good, they were home.

Nate opened the door and grabbed Hank's collar before he could launch himself at her.

"Hi, Brenna," he said. "You're up early."

She shrugged, trying to appear casual. "It's such a nice day I thought I'd borrow Hank and go to the state park for a w . . ."

"Don't say it!" Nate warned.

". . . walk," she finished. Hank went berserk, jumping in circles, forcing Nate to let go of his collar just as Brenna knew he would.

"You realize you have to take him now," he said. He reached inside the door and handed her Hank's leash.

"I know," she said. "Sit, Hank."

Hank stood on his hind legs and hopped.

"Hank, sit," Nate said in a stern voice.

The golden dog danced around in a circle. He was so excited he was wagging from head to toe. Brenna laughed at Nate's chagrinned expression.

"Sit, Hank, sit." Brenna bent over to reach for his collar and Hank licked her chin and cheek. She snapped the leash to his collar. She wiped her face on her shoulder. "Thanks, buddy."

She led Hank to her Jeep and opened the door for him to leap up into the passenger's seat. She felt her shoulders ease as she was almost home free. She turned to walk around to the driver's side and found Nate leaning against her front fender.

"So, how about that game last night?" he asked.

"I didn't see . . ." Brenna trailed off. He knew she hadn't seen the baseball game because of her date, so why was he asking her about it?

"I'm not sure I liked the look of the visiting team," he said. His arms were crossed over his chest in a look of disapproval.

A small smile lifted the corners of Brenna's lips. So it was baseball euphemisms for dating? All righty then.

"I don't know," she said. "I thought they suited up pretty nicely and played a fair game."

"No personal fouls, then?" he asked.

"None." She grinned.

He shoved off of the side of the Jeep and looked down at her. His gray eyes were intense. "Just so you know I would have no problem ejecting a player from the game if need be."

"I appreciate that," she said. "But we're still in tryouts, so no worries."

He grinned, and Brenna got light-headed. No man should have that sort of impact when he smiled, but she figured Nate did it so rarely it was like catching a glimpse of the aurora borealis. Stunning.

He opened the door for her and she climbed in beside Hank and got a big slurp up the side of her face.

"Have a nice walk," he said. "And since we never got to have our conversation about your nosing into the Parker murder last night, we can do that when you get back."

Hank barked and wagged and Brenna could have sworn he understood and was agreeing.

She said nothing, deciding to remain noncommittal. With a wave, she put the Jeep in gear and headed down the drive toward the main road. She wondered if Nate was feeling protective of her dating Dom. And if so, was he protective because he liked her himself or just because they were friends?

Hank had his head out the window, the breeze fluffing his blond tresses while his tail thumped a steady rhythm against her shoulder.

There had been moments when she was so sure that Nate liked her as more than a neighbor, but then again, he never said or did anything that confirmed the feeling. She wasn't willing to make an idiot of herself to find out.

"Best to let it lie. Right, Hank?"

He barked, and again she got the feeling he understood.

She drove through the center of town and on past rolling hills and farm fields. Julie Harper lived on a lonely stretch of road, the kind where passersby wondered what people did for a living that they lived so far away from town. Her old farmhouse was nestled on three sides by the state park, making Brenna's fib to Nate not an outright lie.

She parked the Jeep along the side of the road, hung a water bottle on a carrier around her neck, and pocketed her keys. She took Hank's leash and led him toward a path in the woods. Hank pulled her along the pine-needle-encrusted ground with his nose to the earth.

They went up the hill to a break in the trees, which overlooked the farm below. Brenna stopped to rest on a rock and gaze at Julie's house. There was a car in the driveway, and according to Ruby, Julie hadn't left her house in days. There was no movement around the house and Brenna wondered if Julie was still asleep.

She briefly debated whether she should forge ahead with her plan. Was it really any of her business if Julie had been the one who killed Clue? But then, she thought about Tara and how desperately sad she had looked the night before. And she remembered how she felt when she had been wrongly accused of theft at the gallery in Boston. She would have really liked to have had someone asking questions for her.

With her mind made up, Brenna unclipped Hank's collar and led him down the slope toward the farmhouse. She had brought one of his tennis balls, and when she was within reach, she threw it overhand as far as she could.

Hank did an exuberant leap and bounded down the slope after it. The ball landed up on the back porch, and true to his fetching nature, Hank went right up onto the porch after it.

"Hank, come back," Brenna yelled. Of course, he didn't.

Instead, he dropped the ball and barked as if to say, "Come and get it!"

"Hank!" She tried to make her voice sound exasperated, when in fact she was so happy she wanted to kiss him.

She was halfway across the lawn when the back door opened. *Yes!* She was going to get a chance to talk to Julie.

The door opened wider, but instead of Julie coming out, Hank went inside and the door shut behind him.

Chapter 12

Brenna broke into a run. She stomped up onto the back porch, calling, "Hank!"

No one came to the door. She tried the knob, but it was locked.

"Hey, that's my dog," she called as she pounded on the door. No one answered, and Hank, who usually went mental at the sound of knocking, was terrifyingly silent.

Oh, my God, she thought as she went into a full-blown panic. I borrowed Nate's dog for a covert operation and now I've gotten him locked in a house with a killer. How could I have been so stupid?

She pounded on the door again. She kicked over the doormat, looking for a hidden key. There was nothing but some dirt.

She began to pace the porch, hoping to find something to use to smash the window. A flowerpot with a sickly looking geranium sat on the top step of the stairs.

She snatched it up and was about to heave it at the window, when the door opened.

"Can I help you?" asked a young woman. She had a severe case of bedhead and was wearing a fluffy pink bathrobe with matching bunny slippers.

"I . . . uh . . . I think your flower needs some water," Brenna said as she lowered the pot back to the step. "And I think you have my dog."

Hank trotted back through the gap in the open door. He had a big rawhide chew in his mouth, and Brenna could swear he was grinning at her.

Her heart rate slowed and she took a deep breath.

"I gave him a rawhide bone," the woman said. "I hope that's okay. My Buster died a few months ago, and I had a bunch for him . . ." She broke off with a sob.

Brenna hadn't thought she could feel much worse, but now she felt like something that should be scraped off the bottom of a shoe.

"Oh, don't cry, it's all right," she said.

"No, it's not all right." Julie sat down on the top step.

Hank lay down beside her and worked his rawhide, and Julie absently patted his head.

Brenna studied the woman before her. Her pink bathrobe had finger trails of Cheetos residue on it. One of her bunny slippers was missing an ear. Beneath the robe, she wore a Hello Kitty nightdress, which appeared to have spots of melted chocolate on it. Her long brown hair was limp and lank and Brenna wondered when she had last run a comb through it.

"Having a rough day?" she asked as she sat on the other side of Hank.

"Rough day, rough week, rough life," Julie said.

"Can I help?" Brenna asked, not knowing how she possibly could but feeling as if she should offer anyway.

"You can't help me," Julie said, shoving her hair out of

her eyes. "Unless you can bring someone back from the dead."

Her laugh was bitter and a little chilling. Brenna wondered if she should invent a sudden appointment and scram. But she had come so far, even Hank had risked so much to get her here, she hated to be a big chicken now.

"What do you mean?" she asked.

Julie's pale brown eyes snapped to hers. "You know what I mean."

"No, I don't."

"Well, you're the only one then," Julie said. "Oh, no, not again."

Julie lurched to her feet and made a dash for the door. She didn't make it. Instead, she dropped to her knees and vomited into the flowerpot.

Both Brenna and Hank looked away. No wonder the flower was all wilted and smelled bad. Brenna wiped her fingers on her pants.

"I'll just go get you a cool cloth," she offered while Julie continued to retch.

In the kitchen, which was surprisingly tidy, she found a sunshine yellow dishcloth, which she held under the tap and then wrung out. She hurried back outside and handed it to Julie, who was leaning limply against the porch rail.

"Thanks," she said and held it to her face and neck.

"I'm sorry, I didn't realize you were ill," Brenna said.

"I'm not," Julie said. "I don't have anything that thirty more weeks of getting fat won't cure."

Brenna looked at her curiously, and then it clicked. "You're pregnant."

Julie put one finger on her nose and pointed at Brenna with the other. Then she dry heaved again.

Brenna waited until she was finished and helped her to sit on the top step. Then she sat down hard beside her.

"And no, the father isn't going to make an honest woman of me," Julie said. "He can't, because he's dead."

"I'm sorry," Brenna said. Her sympathy felt horribly inadequate given the complexities of this woman's life.

"You heard about the murder in town?" she asked. Brenna nodded. "That was the father."

"How awful."

"Eh," Julie said. "In the big picture, he got what was coming to him. He was a textbook mother-is-a-whore-therefore-I-hate-all-women sort of man. I'm sure he twisted up that little blonde he was found in bed with into a million knots and she just unraveled. Lord knows, I thought about killing him often enough."

"But you didn't," Brenna said.

"No," Julie said. "I've been too ill with morning sickness to be upright for more than five minutes, never mind take someone's head off with a hacksaw."

"His head wasn't sawed off."

"Really?" Julie asked. "Huh, that's what I heard."

"He was stabbed in the chest," Brenna said.

"How do you know?" Julie asked. Her eyes were narrowed with suspicion.

Brenna decided to come clean. "No one told me. I saw him. I'm the one who found him."

"Oh." Julie sucked in a breath. "Now I recognize you. You're Brenna from Vintage Papers. I've seen you around town."

Brenna nodded.

"Kind of a magnet for dead bodies, aren't you?"

Brenna frowned. "I don't know that I'd say that."

"All the same, it might be best if you go," Julie said. She cupped her belly with her hands. "This is all I have left of him, the product of a midnight booty call I never should have answered, but now, I'm glad I did. It's pitiful, but I think I will love that SOB until the day I die."

Hank and Brenna left Julie enjoying the sunshine on her porch, at least until she threw up again. Despite what Julie said, Brenna had to wonder—if she found Clue in bed with another woman, especially now that she was pregnant with his child, would she be enraged enough to kill him?

It was hard to imagine, given how weak she'd been from barfing, but rage could do amazing things.

They tromped back through the woods and Brenna mulled the situation over in her mind. They broke through the trees toward her Jeep and saw an old, rusty pickup truck tucked in behind it. *Uh-oh.*

Leaning against her vehicle with his ankles crossed and his arms folded over his chest was Nate.

"Did you want to come with us?" Brenna asked. "We just finished."

"No, but it occurred to me after you left that it was odd for you to drive across town to the state park when we live on Morse Point Lake, the prettiest hiking spot in the area."

"I like change," Brenna said.

"Or, more accurately, you're up to something," he said.

"So suspicious," she said.

"Where did Hank get the new rawhide?" he asked.

"You couldn't have buried that?" Brenna asked Hank. He wagged. As if sensing they would be here awhile, he lay down in the grass and began to work in earnest on the chew.

"Talk to me," Nate said.

"What do you want to know?" Brenna asked. "Am I butting in to the investigation? Yes. Am I planning to stop? Uh . . . no."

"Brenna, I appreciate that you want to help, but have you forgotten what happened last April?" he asked. He shoved off of the side of the Jeep and began to pace. "You could have gotten yourself killed."

"But I didn't," she said.

He stopped pacing and stood in front of her. She suspected he knew he was looming and using his height to emphasize his point, but she refused to back up.

"Why are you doing this?"

She didn't answer. If anyone could understand why, it was Nate.

"All right, I know you feel empathetic to anyone who is going through what you went through in Boston," he said. "But that doesn't mean you have to jump in and put yourself in harm's way to help them. You could just offer her moral support, you know, bring her flowers or bake her some brownies. Your brownies are mood elevators, I swear."

Brenna gave him a flat stare.

"Oh, all right," he said. "You're not going to stop, are you?"

"Nope."

"Then you have to promise me that the next time you go barging in on a suspect, you will take me or Tenley or Matt with you. At the very least, you should let us know where you are and what you're doing. That's just common sense."

Brenna frowned. She couldn't really argue with that reasoning, although she might have tried if he hadn't just praised her brownies so highly.

"All right," she agreed.

"Shake on it," he said and held out his hand.

"You're being ridiculous," she said but she took his large hand in hers and pumped it up and down. "I promise."

"Good," he said. His shoulders dropped down from around his ears and he looked visibly relieved. "So, what did you find out from Julie the stalker?"

"How did you know about her?"

"I'd have to be a much bigger recluse than I am to have

missed that news," he said. "Ed Johnson has run her photo with the story that Clue took a restraining order out against her no less than three times in the *Courier*."

"Well, it's more complicated than it seems," Brenna said. "She's pregnant, and according to her, the baby is Clue's. Apparently, the restraining order only went one way."

"Oh," he said.

"She might have found him with Tara and stabbed him in a jealous rage," Brenna said. "Goodness knows, he gave her enough reason to, but I'm not convinced."

"Given that she hasn't been arrested, I'd say Chief Barker isn't either," Nate said. "Now what?"

"I go to work and see if there is any more news," she said. "Since you're here, do you mind taking Hank home?"

"Not at all," he said. "But remember your promise."

"I will," she said. "I won't do anything without letting someone know."

Brenna climbed into her Jeep while Nate opened up the passenger door of his truck for Hank. He was watching her, his gray eyes intent upon her face. Brenna got the feeling he had something he wanted to say, but then he looked away.

She honked as she pulled out and waved out the half-open window. She saw him raise his hand in return in the rearview mirror and wondered what he might have said.

When she arrived at Vintage Papers, she had worked out at least three different variations of a conversation in which Nate confessed to being in love with her. She knew it was silly, but it was an amusing daydream nonetheless.

Tenley had just unlocked the doors when she arrived, and Brenna made her way straight for the coffeepot in the break room.

"How was it?" Tenley asked.

Brenna looked confused. How did Tenley know about her conversation with Nate?

"The date? With Dom?" Tenley prodded.

"Oh, that," Brenna said.

"Yes, that. Why do you think I've been calling your cell phone all morning? It'd be nice if you'd answer it, by the way."

"Oh, I forgot it at the cabin," Brenna said. "I took Hank for a long walk by Julie Harper's this morning."

"You *have* been busy," Tenley said. "When Nate gets back, he's going to be pleased at how much attention you've given Hank."

"He is back," Brenna said. "He arrived last night right before my date with Dom."

"No!"

"Yes!"

Tenley ran her eyes over the shop. No one had come in yet. She pointed to the worktable in back and said, "Sit and speak."

Brenna did. This was the joy of a best girlfriend. She could tell Tenley anything and her friend was right there, feeling everything she felt and thinking everything she'd thought.

At the end of it, Tenley asked, "What do you think Nate wanted to say to you?"

"No idea," Brenna said. "Maybe it's just wishful thinking on my part."

"Maybe, but I don't think so."

The bells on the front door chimed. Brenna glanced up, expecting the Porter sisters to arrive in full interrogation mode, but was surprised to see Tara and Tiffany Montgomery.

"Good morning," Tenley greeted them. She took Tara's hands in hers. "How are you?"

Tara was wearing a pretty periwinkle sundress with navy sandals, while Tiffany was in a tailored linen sheath in a deep rose. Despite the pretty dresses, the two women looked haggard, even more so than they had at dinner the night before.

"I'm holding up," Tara said. "In fact, I've decided to attend the concert on the green tonight."

"Good for you," Tenley cheered her. "The brass band from the Elks Lodge is playing and what they lack in skill, they make up for in enthusiasm."

Tiffany looked alarmed.

"It's true," Brenna agreed. "I've never heard anything quite like it."

"Oh, I don't know," Tiffany said. "Your father would rather we keep to ourselves until we can go back to Boston."

"I'm not going back to Boston," Tara said. "I'm staying here and I'm marrying Jake."

"Tara, you have to see reason," her mother pleaded. "Jake hasn't spoken to you since that awful morning. He doesn't believe you."

"He does believe me, but his best friend was killed. He needs time to think it through." Tara's eyes flooded and she looked ready to weep.

"Well, the best spot in the park is under the fourth maple tree on the south side. The tuba player faces the other way, so you don't get the full blast and you're within ten feet of the Italian ice booth," Tenley said.

Tara gave her a lopsided smile.

"Brenna and I will be there on a blanket and you're welcome to join us," Tenley said and then glanced at Tiffany. "All of you."

"Really?" Tara asked Brenna.

Tenley was a big fat liar—they had no plan to sit on a blanket there—but Brenna figured this was one of Tenley's causes for the greater good, and like any worthy gal pal she backed her friend's fib without hesitation.

"Absolutely," she said.

"It's very kind of you, but I think Tara needs to stay out of sight," Tiffany said.

"No," Tara said. "I didn't do anything wrong and I am not going to hide and act as if I did."

"But . . ."

"No," Tara said. Her eyes were clear and her chin was set at a determined angle, as if she were hoping someone would take a swing at her so she could knock them back. "You don't have to go, Mother, but I do. I'll see you two at seven then."

With a twirl of periwinkle she turned and swept out the door, leaving a bemused Tiffany to follow in her wake.

"So, we're going to the concert?" Brenna asked.

"Great way to people watch, don't you think?"

"Or murderer watch, depending upon how you look at it," Brenna said. "How close are we to the funnel cake guy?"

"He's on the other side of the Italian ice booth," Tenley said.

"Okay, I'm in," Brenna said. "Let's hope our killer decides to show up as well."

Chapter 13

Brenna wasn't sure if it was a trombone or a baboon making such a racket. Since there was no sign of a baboon in the crowd, she had to figure it was the trombone; either way, she was thinking the funnel cakes were going to have to go in her ears instead of her mouth to save her sanity.

She and Tenley spread their well-worn log cabin quilt under the fourth tree as promised. She went for funnel cakes while Tenley hunted down lemonades. The green was rapidly filling up with families and couples. The Italian ice booth had a line of children, and Sharon Liu, the photographer for the *Courier*, was snapping pictures as the Elks Lodge band continued warming up in the gazebo.

The June air was warm with a hint of the sticky humidity that would be coming their way in the next month. Large rolling clouds billowed to the east, while the sun made its descent in the west. If it weren't for the recent murder in the bucolic town, Brenna would have said this was a picture-perfect moment.

She sat cross-legged on the blanket, holding her hot funnel cake on its paper plate. She was just leaning in to take her first bite of powdery sugar goodness when she felt a sudden change in the festive mood. Loud voices became muted as a whisper moved through the crowd, gossiping in everyone's ears in a mass version of the telephone game.

Brenna didn't have to look up to know that Tara had arrived. She sighed as she put her funnel cake down and turned to greet the young woman. As usual, she was bookended by her parents, with Tyler throwing narrow-eyed looks at anyone who might snub his baby.

Brenna hugged Tara and shook hands with her parents. The whisper moved again when Tara sat down. Brenna could see the crowd parting to reveal Jake on the other side of the green. He didn't acknowledge Tara but kept his gaze on the gazebo as if the band were already playing instead of shifting in their seats watching the show on the lawn before them unfold.

Tenley arrived holding two icy lemonades and Brenna breathed a sigh of relief. Being Tenley Morse, born into the family for which Morse Point was named, she carried more social clout than Brenna. When she handed Brenna the lemonades and then hugged Tara, the whisper reached a fevered pitch and then hushed.

Tenley's parents didn't attend the concerts on the green, which made the townsfolk smile even more favorably upon Tenley since they felt she was the most grounded member of the Morse family, which Brenna knew to be true. It gave Tenley quite a bit of power in town, which she was not above using to Tara's benefit.

Brenna was glad. Despite her brave words, Tara looked nervous. Her eyes kept darting to the spot where Jake was sitting, and it looked as if a little part of her died every time he didn't look back.

"Well, then, have some funnel cake," Brenna said and shoved her uneaten sweet into Tara's hands.

Tyler and Tiffany sat in folding chairs behind them, like well-heeled gargoyles.

"This should be fun," Brenna said to Tenley.

Tenley grinned at her. The stout conductor walked to the front of the gazebo and rapped his baton on a music stand three times. All eyes turned to the stage, and in a deafening blast of bleats and screeches, the concert began.

Brenna felt both of the Montgomerys stiffen beside her. She was pretty sure they'd never heard anything like this in Boston.

The Elks Lodge band was made up of grown-ups who had once been in the Morse Point High School marching band. They called themselves the Dirty Dozen and wore a uniform of black pants and shoes with white shirts and black blazers with red lapels and black bow ties. The instruments consisted of a collection of trumpets, tubas, cornets, and trombones, with one percussionist who sat in the back with an assortment of cymbals, triangles, and a large timpani drum.

What they lacked in finesse they made up for in sheer determination. As they wailed away at "The Saints Go Marching In" a troupe of little girls hopped up and danced in front of the gazebo, twirling their pretty dresses until they fell down, dizzy and giggling. It was impossible not to smile, and Brenna noticed even Tyler Montgomery tapping his foot on the downbeat.

The band played for an hour and ended their show with a rousing rendition of John Philip Sousa's "Stars and Stripes Forever." For their effort, they got a standing ovation from the crowd and free funnel cake.

Tenley and Brenna were shaking out their blanket when Maya Hopper approached.

"I can't believe you'd bring her here," Maya hissed.

Tenley raised her eyebrows and looked down her nose at Maya in a spot-on impression of her mother. Tenley's mother could wilt a person with a look from fifty paces.

"I can't imagine what you mean," Tenley said. Meaning, of course, that if Maya had a brain in her head, she would back away now before Tenley shredded her like a sheet of inferior paper.

The Porter sisters appeared out of the crowd and edged close to Brenna, one on each side, so as not to miss a word of the scene.

"Maya has an ulterior motive," Marie whispered from behind her cup of watermelon ice.

"She used to go out with Jake, but then he dumped her for Tara," Ella said around a mouthful of funnel cake.

"She's a murderer," Maya said. As if aware that all eyes were upon her, she tossed her brown black hair over her shoulders and cranked up the melodrama a notch by proclaiming, "You will pay for what you've done, Tara Montgomery, and not with your daddy's money."

The Montgomerys stepped forward to shield Tara, but she held out her arms, stopping them.

"No, I'm all right," she said. "She's only saying what everyone else is thinking."

Her eyes searched the crowd, and Brenna knew she was looking for Jake. He stepped forward, pushing past Maya.

"I don't think that," he said.

Tara gave him a faint, hopeful smile.

Turning his back to her and facing the crowd, he cleared his throat and said in a voice that was low but no less forceful, "Tara Montgomery is innocent. She is one of the kindest people I have ever known, and I know that she didn't harm my friend. If anyone has a problem with that, you can take it up with me."

A low murmur moved across the lawn.

"You're a fool, Jake Haywood," Maya snapped. She spun on her heel and made her way through the crowd. When Bart Thompson didn't move fast enough, she knocked his Italian ice into his tie-dyed shirt, leaving him to gasp and stutter while hopping from foot to foot from the sudden blast of cold. Maya didn't stop to apologize.

Brenna met Tenley's gaze and raised her eyebrows as if to say, Another suspect? Tenley gave her a small nod of understanding.

The crowd dispersed, and when Jake would have left, Tara stepped forward and grabbed his arm. He didn't meet her gaze but stared down at her hand on his elbow.

"Jake." She said his name with a voice full of hope. "Thank you."

He finally glanced up at her. He took her hand off of his arm and said, "Just because I don't think you killed him, doesn't mean that I believe you didn't sleep with him."

Tara stepped back from him, looking as if she'd been slapped.

Jake looked sick to his stomach. "Why was he in your bed, Tara? Why?"

Her eyes filled with tears and her voice cracked when she said, "I don't know."

Jake turned away and stomped across the park toward the Haywood garage.

Tara broke down into sobs. Brenna, Tenley, and the Montgomerys all took a step in her direction but Margie Haywood beat them to it. She pulled Tara into her arms and let her cry on her shoulder while she patted her back just like she did the kids at Morse Point Elementary when they got a boo-boo.

"There there," she said. "It'll be all right."

"But he thinks . . ." Tara's voice trailed off as she dissolved into sobs.

"I know," Margie said. She glanced at the Montgomerys over Tara's head and a look of understanding passed between them. "I'm sorry to say this, but if Jake doesn't believe you, what kind of a life will you have together? Maybe, honey, it's all for the best."

"But I love him and he loves me," Tara sobbed.

Brenna felt her own throat get tight, and she glanced at Tenley, who looked choked up as well. The Porter sisters were huddled together and had tears running down their cheeks. Marie gave a healthy blast into her handkerchief.

"Give it some time," Margie said. "Just give it some time."

"Thank you," Tara said as she stepped back from Margie. "But I don't want time. I want Jake."

With a sob, she dashed off across the green. Tyler and Tiffany exchanged a glance and bolted after her.

Tenley put her hand on Margie's arm. "That was nice of you."

"It's that nursing thing," Margie said with a wave of her hand. "I hate to see anyone suffering."

"How is Jake holding up?" Brenna asked as she joined them.

"Oh, you know Jake," she said. Her forehead creased with a line of maternal worry, probably deeper now than it had ever been before. "He's the strong silent type, like his father. I'm trying to protect him as best I can, but it's hard when they grow up."

"Has Chief Barker been to see him?" Brenna asked. Tenley shot her a look, but Brenna kept her eyes on Margie.

"Several times," Margie said. "It's a bad business, Clue being found in bed with his fiancée, but both Mr. Haywood and I can vouch for Jake's whereabouts. He was home with us all night."

"Well, that's a relief," Marie said as she joined their little group.

"Everyone knows Jake would never harm a fly," Ella said.

Margie gave them a closed-lipped smile, and Brenna could tell that she was still worried about her son and would be until the murderer was caught.

"If you need anything," Tenley said, "you let us know."

"Thank you, dear," Margie said. With a small wave she turned and followed in the wake of her son.

"Poor thing," Ella said. "The sun rises and sets on that boy of hers. This has got to be killing her and John."

Marie raised her eyebrows at her sister.

"Oh, sorry, poor choice of words," Ella said.

"I'll say," Marie said. "You know who young Tara reminds me of?"

"Who?" Ella asked.

"Me," Marie said in a voice that cracked with emotion. "In fact, her love for Jake is so very much like my love for John Henry."

Ella rolled her eyes. "Oh, for heaven's sake! John Henry thought you were me."

"He did not," Marie argued. "We were tragic lovers like Romeo and Juliet. I . . ."

Whatever Marie had been about to say was cut off by Ella shoving a piece of funnel cake in her mouth.

"There," Ella said. "That's better."

Marie looked outraged as she furiously chewed. Brenna and Tenley had to turn away before they burst out laughing.

"See you at the shop," Brenna called, without waiting for an answer.

The crowd had thinned. Most people were standing in clumps, catching up on each other's lives while their children ran amuck.

Brenna dodged a redheaded girl chasing the middle Page boy, recognizable as one of Lillian's by his shock of unruly black hair and glasses. The girl giving chase was wearing a tiara and brandishing a wand with a sparkly star on the end.

"I turned you into a frog!" she was yelling. "You have to stop and let me kiss you now."

The look the Page boy cast over his shoulder was one of sheer terror and he picked up his pace to a flat-out run. Brenna made a mental note to tell Lillian at their next decoupage class that as far as girls went, her boys, at least this one, were safely immune.

Tenley nudged Brenna with her elbow and pointed across the street. Standing in front of Vintage Papers, having an intense discussion, were the Montgomerys and Chief Barker.

"Oh!" Brenna glanced both ways and then dashed across the street with Tenley right behind her.

They were just stepping onto the walk, when Mr. Montgomery started to yell. "We have been more than cooperative! Now I demand that you let us take our daughter back to Boston, where she won't be forced to suffer such humiliation."

"I appreciate that this has been difficult," Chief Barker said. His voice was low and soothing, his Massachusetts accent subdued, and Brenna suspected he was trying to calm Mr. Montgomery down. "But I'm afraid Tara is still a suspect, and until we can determine exactly what happened that night, she will need to remain in town."

"This is ludicrous!" Mr. Montgomery railed. "Her bridesmaids have all been allowed to leave. There's no reason Tara should still be here. You'll be hearing from my attorney in the morning, and if you don't let us leave this godforsaken backwater, then I will sue you—in fact, I'll sue this whole bloody town!"

He took both Tara and Tiffany by their elbows and led

them down the street toward the Morse Point Inn. A hush filled Main Street as people watched them go.

"Well, that's not going to make them any friends," Tenley said, and Brenna could tell she was miffed on behalf of her town.

"He's upset," Brenna said.

"You think?" Chief Barker asked.

She felt Chief Barker's gaze upon her face and turned to face him. She wondered if this was where she got her "stop being a buttinsky" lecture.

"Did Nate talk to you?" he asked. He ran his thumb and forefinger over his thick gray mustache in a mannerism Brenna recognized as one he made when he was striving for patience.

"Yes, he did," she said.

"And?"

"And I understand completely," she said. She wondered if she was being vague enough.

Tenley was glancing between them as if she were trying to figure out what they were talking about but didn't want to be rude by asking.

"It's for your own safety," he said.

"I know," she said.

"I'm glad we've reached this agreement."

He smiled at her and Brenna suddenly knew exactly what Mrs. Barker saw in him. His grin was engaging and a little bit mischievous.

"Have a good night, ladies," he said. He tipped the brim of his gray, wide-brimmed hat with the Morse Point police logo on the front and walked down the sidewalk toward the Haywood garage.

As Tenley unlocked the front door to Vintage Papers, she frowned at Brenna and asked, "What was that all about?"

"Me staying out of the murder case," Brenna said.

Tenley just looked at her.

"Yeah, I know," Brenna said. "You'll notice I made no promises."

"Uh-huh," Tenley said. "Very clever."

Brenna noted her sarcasm, but let it pass. "You know what I keep thinking about?"

"I'm afraid to ask," Tenley said. They locked the front door behind them and went into the break room at the back of the shop where they had stored their purses.

Tenley opened the cupboard and pulled out both bags, handing Brenna hers and shouldering her own.

"When Jake asked Tara why Clue was in her bed, she genuinely didn't have a clue."

"Ugh. How long have you been waiting to say that?" Tenley asked her.

"A couple of days," Brenna admitted.

"You have a dark side," Tenley said, but she was smiling.

"I know, forgive me," she said as they stepped out the back door. They had parked behind the shop to give others more room to park on the street.

"So, what is going through that brain of yours now?"

"What if we could get Tara to remember what happened that night?"

Tenley's eyes went wide. "Don't you think she's tried?"

"Yes, with no success. At the concert, I heard Tiffany and Tyler talking about hiring someone to put her through hypnosis."

"That might work," Tenley said, but she sounded as dubious as Brenna felt.

"What if she retraces her steps? We could take her back through the events of that night and maybe she'd remember a few details."

"You could be on to something," Tenley said.

"So," Brenna said with a grin. "What are you doing to-morrow night?"

"Going out with the girls, apparently."

Chapter 14

Brenna called Tara and she eagerly agreed to give it a try. Brenna could tell by her tone of voice that she was desperate to remember what happened that night. They agreed to meet up at Vintage Papers that evening. In the meantime, Brenna had decided to pop in on Lisa Sutton's family and see if they could tell her anything about the girl's whereabouts. She knew it was a long shot, but maybe Lisa knew something about Clue that would help them out.

The Sutton residence was in a planned community called Chestnut Hill on the west side of town. Built in the 1970s, this collection of raised ranches was a mini neighborhood unto itself.

In the center was Chestnut Hill Park, with a huge playground, basketball and tennis courts, and a field big enough for soccer games. The houses spread out from around the park in a circular pattern, and after driving around and doubling back a few times, Brenna found the Sutton home.

It was white with green trim; neatly pruned hedges

hemmed the house and an American flag flapped in the light breeze from its holder above the front door.

Brenna parked her Jeep in the drive and made her way up the walkway toward the door. Three steps up and she rang the bell. She could hear it echo inside the house and a dog, small from the yappy sound of the bark, answered with a chorus of yips.

"Hush, Jasmine," a voice commanded. The dog kept barking.

The large wooden door swung in and a gray-haired, middle-aged woman, wearing jeans and a cotton blouse, peered out at her. She had a little white dog, presumably Jasmine, tucked under her arm.

"May I help you?" she asked. She didn't smile.

"Hi, I hope so. I'm Brenna Miller. I'm looking for Mrs. Sutton, Lisa's mother."

The woman stiffened. "I'm her mother. Is there news? Have you seen her?"

Brenna was taken aback by the desperation in the woman's hazel eyes. Mrs. Sutton studied Brenna's face, and then her shoulders slumped. "You'd think after three years, I'd give up hope, but I just can't."

"I'm sorry," Brenna said. "I didn't mean to upset you. I'm a friend of the girl who is accused of killing Clue Parker, and I just wondered if Lisa knew anything about Clue that might help solve his murder."

"I really couldn't say," Mrs. Sutton said. "As far as I know, no one has heard from her since she left. The rumor is that she went to be a chef in Boston, but why wouldn't she tell us? My husband and I tried to find her. We even hired a private detective, but he didn't find anything. It's like she vanished into thin air."

Jasmine wiggled in her arms, trying to get to Brenna. Mrs. Sutton gestured for Brenna to follow her into the house. They stood on a tiled foyer with a short flight of stairs leading down and another leading up. Mrs. Sutton led the way up the stairs into a large sitting room, kept light by the bay window that looked out onto the front yard.

"Can I get you anything?" Mrs. Sutton asked.

"No, thank you," Brenna said. A hutch stood against the far wall. It was covered in pictures of a pretty brunette girl, Lisa, from infancy to her early twenties. Her infectious smile was captured by the camera in almost every pose, except for one. It was black and white and sat on the far corner of the shelf. It was a profile picture of Lisa and she looked pensive as if she had just received terrible news and was trying to decide what to do.

Brenna was drawn to the picture. She wanted to know what the young woman was thinking, what decision she was trying to make. She noticed Lisa was fingering a small angel pendant worked in a delicate gold.

"That's the last picture ever taken of her," Mrs. Sutton said from behind her. "My son Tommy took it for his photography class at school. The next day Lisa was gone."

"Why?" Brenna asked. "Why did she leave and never return?"

"The gossips say that she was in love with Jake and that he rejected her because of his friendship with Clue. People think she ran away because she was heartbroken, but I don't believe that."

"No?"

"I think Jake was in love with her, too," Mrs. Sutton said. "What's more, I think Jake would have left with her if she asked him."

Brenna sank down onto the burgundy sofa while Mrs. Sutton sat in the matching armchair across from her.

"What makes you think that?"

"I overheard them together," Mrs. Sutton said. "I walked in on them while they were out on our sunporch. They didn't hear me, but I heard them. I saw the way Jake looked at her and I heard her ask him to leave Morse Point and run away with her where they could be together, away from Clue. When I asked her about it, she said it was just silly talk."

Brenna was stunned. She hadn't seen this coming.

"Did you ever ask Jake about it?"

"Oh, yes, he was devastated. She left him her angel." Mrs. Sutton motioned to the pendant Lisa held in the somber picture. "No note. No explanation. Just the angel."

"Mrs. Sutton, what do you think happened?" she asked.

"I think Clue Parker found out what they were planning, and I think he chased her away. I never liked him. He was cruel, and he bragged about how no woman could resist him. He would have hated having Lisa dump him for his friend," she said. Her lips trembled a bit. "That's why I was hoping with him dead, maybe she would come home."

"Did you tell Chief Barker all of this?" Brenna asked.

"Oh, yes, when she went missing, I told him everything," Mrs. Sutton said. "He's a good man and he questioned Clue mercilessly, but Clue denied knowing anything about Lisa's whereabouts. And Jake, well, he had the angel. He was about as heartbroken as I was."

"I'm so sorry, Mrs. Sutton, I can't imagine how hard it must be for you to not know where she is," Brenna said.

Mrs. Sutton patted a stray gray hair back into place as if trying to restore order to her world. "Thank you. If you hear anything about Lisa, anything at all, will you let me know?"

"Absolutely," Brenna said. "I promise."

She left the Sutton house, after rubbing Jasmine's tummy, and headed back to town. Mrs. Sutton's story certainly checked out with what Marie Porter had said about Lisa loving Jake, but the endings were vastly different.

Why had Lisa suddenly left Morse Point? Had Clue threatened her? Again, Brenna thought of the way Clue had looked at Tara on the night of the bachelorette party. It was certainly possible. Had he threatened others? If so, had someone finally had enough and murdered him? It was also a good possibility, but the question was who?

"My mother thinks I'm working on a decoupage project with you," Tara said.

"So, you are," Brenna said, and she pulled Tara over to the worktable where she was gluing on the last few squares of Betty Cartwright's hope chest.

She handed Tara a brayer and motioned for her to roll over the squares she had recently put on. Tara gently ran the brayer and then Brenna handed her a wet cloth to dab up the glue that was pushed out from under the papers.

"You're a natural," Tenley said from the other side of the chest.

Tara gave her a shy smile, and the three of them continued to work in silence until the last square was in place and Tara had rolled over it and dabbed up the excess glue.

They all stood back and studied their work. Brenna had been dubious when she had first conceived the piece but now, she had to admit, it was spectacular.

"Wow," breathed Tara, endearing herself even more to the two women.

"Let's leave it to dry," Brenna said, gathering her materials while Tenley did the same. They rinsed the brushes and washed the bowls and put the glue back in the break room.

"Now I think all of that hard work deserves a nice glass of iced tea at the Fife and Drum, don't you?" Brenna asked Tenley, who promptly excused herself to go freshen up.

"I don't know," Tara said. "I'm nervous."

"Are you afraid people will be nasty and whisper about you?" Brenna asked.

"No," Tara said with a shake of her head. "I think I'm actually getting used to that."

"Then what is it?"

"What if we do all this and I still can't remember?"

"You'll be no worse off than you are now," Brenna said. "But I don't want to pressure you; the decision is yours."

Tara bit her lip while she considered her options. "All right, let's do it."

"'Atta girl," Brenna cheered her, and she smiled.

Twenty minutes later, the three women strolled into the Fife and Drum. The bar was crowded and the faint sound of clattering plates and murmured dinner conversations could just be heard behind the doors to the restaurant beyond.

The interior of the Fife and Drum was dark. Black wainscoting lined the lower walls, with a rich burgundy wallpaper, sporting black fleur-de-lis, was placed atop it. Candles were lit on every table and the waitstaff, which moved at a clip, wore white dress shirts with black vests over black pants.

Matt was behind the bar, dressed in a white dress shirt but with the sleeves rolled up to his elbows, and Tenley led the way there. She slid onto a stool and Tara took the one beside her. Brenna opted to stand.

Matt looked at Tenley and his eyes glowed. "Well, this is a pleasant surprise."

Tenley beamed.

"What can I get you ladies?"

"Iced tea all around," Brenna answered. "We need to keep our wits about us."

"Why would that be?" a low voice drawled from behind her.

Brenna jumped and spun around to find Nate standing right behind her.

"Ah!" She put her hand over her heart. "You scared me."

"Sorry," he said.

Brenna noticed his gray eyes looked amused and not one iota repentant.

"Yeah, right," she said.

"So, what are you ladies up to tonight?" he asked.

"We're re-creating the night of the . . ." Tara began but Brenna interrupted with a fake cough.

"I'm sorry, I didn't catch that," Nate said and leaned closer to Tara.

She gave Brenna a confused look and then said, "The night of the murder."

Nate turned back to Brenna, but this time there was no amusement in his glance.

"Explain," he said.

Brenna looked to Tenley for help, but she and Matt were cozied up talking, while Tara was blinking at her with a wide-eyed innocence that indicated she had no idea what she had just done. *Oy.*

"It's really very simple," Brenna said. "Tara can't remember the events of that night, so we are retracing her steps and hoping to jog her memory."

"How is that butting out?" Nate asked. He ran a hand through his hair, which Brenna knew was not a good sign.

"I'm just trying to help a friend," she said.

"You can't—" Nate started to lecture, but Tara let out a squeak and they both turned to see what had alarmed her.

Standing in the doorway to the bar was Jake. He looked devastated to see Tara, as if he couldn't decide whether to hug her close or run for his life. Brenna realized that no matter what had happened that night, Jake was still very much in love with his bride to be.

He turned to leave, but she called out, "Jake!"

He stopped, waited for a second, and then slowly turned around. Brenna crossed the room in five strides. She wanted to catch him before he changed his mind.

"Jake, listen, we're trying to figure out what happened that night," she said. "Do you want to help us?"

She felt Nate step up behind her. She knew he didn't agree with what she was doing, but she was grateful for his presence at her back.

"I can't," Jake said. "I don't want to know if . . ."

"What? If your worst fears are true?" Nate asked from behind her. "Wouldn't it be better to know?"

"I don't think I could bear it," Jake said.

"What if it goes the other way?" Brenna asked. "What if nothing happened between them and she is innocent?"

The young man sucked a breath through his teeth, as if he'd just suffered a body blow. Brenna suspected he desperately wanted that outcome but was afraid to hope for it.

"Please, Jake," Tara said as she joined their group. "If you ever loved me, help me now. Help me find out what happened that night."

A shudder rippled through his shoulders and he tossed back his head, a gladiator ready to fight to the death.

"All right," he said. "I'm in."

"Where do we start?" Matt asked as he and Tenley joined the group. Brenna noticed that he had his arm draped over her shoulders and she was beaming.

"You're coming, too?" she asked.

"I just got off my shift," he said. "I figure I can act as a stand-in."

"Me, too," Nate volunteered.

"Excellent," Brenna said. "Okay, let's start here. Everyone take your positions from when the bachelorette party started."

"You were behind the bar, flirting with that buxom bridesmaid," Tenley said to Matt. "I can't remember her name."

"Britney," he said, and Tenley frowned. "I remember because she was so not my type. I'm more of a leg man."

Tenley flushed a lovely shade of pink and shooed him back behind the bar.

"Nate, will you stand in for Clue?" Brenna asked. "Tara and Jake were hugging. Go ahead."

Tara and Jake awkwardly stepped into each other's arms. Jake didn't seem to know where to put his hands and Tara kept trying to see his face to make sure he was okay. Finally, she just gave in and hugged him fiercely. Jake leaned his chin down into her hair and took a deep breath. Then he, too, wrapped his arms about her and held her close.

"Okay, now Nate, you look at Tara," Brenna said. He did but she shook her head. "No, look at her as if you don't like her."

Jake and Tara both gave Brenna a questioning glance. Nate glowered at Tara, but it lacked any heat. Still, it made Brenna remember what happened next.

"Now, look at me," she said. Nate did but his gray eyes were warm and she didn't feel the scary shiver that she had when Clue looked at her.

"What are you remembering?" he asked.

"Jake, how did Clue feel about you getting married?" she asked.

"He was okay with it," he said. He didn't meet her gaze and Brenna stared at him with one eyebrow raised.

"How did he feel?" Tara asked, stepping back from Jake.

"Not happy," Jake sighed. "He thought I was crazy to give up my freedom."

"You never told me that," Tara said.

"I didn't want to hurt your feelings," Jake said. "Besides,

I knew I wanted to spend my life with you. I didn't care what he thought."

"I think Clue was more than a little angry about you marrying Tara," Brenna said. "I saw it in his face when he looked at the two of you. It was scary."

Jake blew out a breath as he took this in. "I didn't know."

They were all silent for a moment, and then Nate asked, "What happened next?"

"Clue insulted the bridesmaids," Tenley said.

"Then he apologized," Tara added.

"And we left," Jake finished.

"Okay, then, where to next?" Matt asked.

"The Willow House," all three women answered together.

The women took Brenna's Jeep, while the men climbed into Jake's vintage GTO. It was easy to see the lust in Nate's and Matt's eyes as they climbed into the classic muscle car.

Tenley rolled her eyes at Brenna, as if to say, "Men."

The Willow House was the local college students' hangout and the best place in the area to listen to live music. Occasional bands from Boston passed through, but the majority of it was local talent.

On this night, just like the last time they were here, a live cover band was jamming and the place was packed. Tenley and Brenna made their way to the same table where they had stood that night.

Tenley nudged Brenna with her elbow. "I don't think we really need to revisit the conversation where we discover we're old, do you?"

Brenna glanced at Nate and Matt behind them. "Nope, I don't see a need."

Tara stood beside their table and studied the room in front of them. "Britney was dancing with a whole group of men, while Dana and Marissa watched. I got a phone call—from you."

She pointed to Jake and he said, "Yeah, I remember."

"We sat here drinking coffee, when Dom Cappicola came over and asked Brenna out," Tenley said.

In spite of herself, Brenna felt her face get hot.

"So, that's when it happened," Nate said.

"Moving along," Brenna said. She could feel Nate watching her, but she refused to meet his gaze.

"Then I joined Dana and Marissa," Tara said. "And they said they wanted to go somewhere else, so we followed Britney back to the table."

"And we all agreed to go home," Tenley said.

"Yeah, but it didn't work out that way," Tara said. Her voice was full to the brim with what-ifs, and Brenna took her hand and squeezed it in sympathetic understanding. There was no time to get weepy about what couldn't be changed, however.

"So, what happened next?" Jake asked. He reminded Brenna of a pointer dog, looking for a hunter's fallen bird. He wasn't going to relent until he knew what happened.

"The limo took us back to town," Tara said. "And I went to get out with Brenna and Tenley, but Britney dragged me back into the car and told the driver to take us to the Brass Rail."

Brenna looked at the group. "Next stop the Brass Rail."

They all nodded in agreement and trudged back out to their cars. Brenna watched Nate stroll toward the GTO, and she marveled that he was here with them.

Nate was friendly with Matt, but he didn't know Jake at all. This was so against his reclusive nature that she had to wonder what was motivating him to help them.

Before he climbed into the car, their gazes met over the roof. A small smile lifted the corner of his mouth and he gave his head a small shake. Brenna realized he was here because of her. Out of friendship, or whatever it was that he felt for her.

A grin parted her lips, and he blinked as if temporarily blinded by the wattage before he grinned back.

Brenna climbed into the Jeep to find Tenley watching her.

"What's making you so happy?" she asked.

"I think we might get some answers tonight," Brenna said. "That's all."

"Uh-huh," Tenley grunted, looking out the window at Nate and then back at Brenna. "Sure."

"Do you think so?" Tara asked from the backseat.

Brenna glanced at her in the rearview mirror. She had her fingers laced together almost as if she were praying.

Brenna sobered up immediately. This wasn't about her and Nate. This was about Tara and finding out what happened to her on the night of Clue's murder.

Her eyes met Tara's in the mirror as she pulled out of the lot.

"Yes, I do," she said, hoping for Tara's sake that she was right.

Chapter 15

"I told you so," Tenley said.

"Told me what?" Brenna asked.

The two women stared at the squat little brick building before them.

"That this place is a dump."

Brenna remembered the night of the bachelorette party, when Tenley had called this place a dump; now that seemed overly flattering.

Off the beaten path, the Brass Rail was tucked behind the small industrial section of Morse Point, an area that was home to a self-storage facility, a propane gas distributor, and a trucking company.

The dirt lot was unlined and parking was willy-nilly. Brenna did the best she could and was relieved when Jake pulled up beside her. "You actually went *in* there?" she asked Tara.

"Yeah," Tara said on a heavy sigh.

Motorcycles were parked in a row across the front of

the building. A bouncer the size of a refrigerator stood by the front door, which was open, spilling out rowdy shouts and laughter and jukebox music that maintained a deafening beat mingled with grinding guitar solos.

Jake opened the back door for Tara, while Matt got Tenley's door, leaving Nate to open Brenna's. There was no turning back now.

"Talk us through what you remember, Tara," Brenna said. "You were the only one of us here that night, so we can't help you."

"The limo pulled up here," she said, and she walked over to the motorcycles. "We tumbled out. Dana actually fell into the dirt and Britney laughed at her. Clue was working the door."

Her voice grew soft and she gave Jake a worried look.

"It's okay," he said with a nod of his head. "Keep going."

Tara took a deep breath. "Clue helped Dana up and then walked us into the bar."

"Let's do it then," Jake said. He took Tara by the elbow and led her up to the bouncer.

"Hey, man." The bouncer recognized Jake and they traded a complicated handshake that started normally, included some backhand action, and ended with them pounding one fist atop another. "I'm sorry about Clue, man. That was messed up."

"Yeah, thanks," Jake said.

The bouncer squinted at Tara, but Jake hustled her past him before he could recognize her. The bouncer nodded as the rest of them passed through the door.

"I think I'm offended that we weren't carded," Tenley whispered to Brenna.

"It's because we're with Jake and he's a regular," Brenna said.

"That's our story and we're sticking to it," Tenley whispered back.

Tara turned to face them. She raised her voice to a low yell to be heard over the twangy dance music coming out of the jukebox. "This is where Marissa took Dana to the ladies' room to clean up, and Britney went to dance with some scary biker guy."

"Do you see him here?" Brenna asked, hoping they could ask him some questions.

Tara scanned the room and shook her head.

"We'll be them," Matt volunteered.

Without waiting for an answer, he led Tenley out onto the dance floor, which was a small square of wooden-looking linoleum wedged between two pool tables.

"Does that mean we have to be the bridesmaids?" Nate asked her.

"Ick. No," she said. "Let's just follow Tara and see what she remembers."

"I remember I stood here for a little while, feeling very out of place," Tara said.

"Understatement of the year," Nate whispered to Brenna, and she hushed him.

Tara studied the room around her, but Brenna could tell she wasn't seeing the room as it was now, but rather as it had been that night.

"I decided I'd be safer by the bar," she said. "It was crowded, so I sat at the end by the wall."

The same seat was empty now, so they followed her as she made her way toward it. It was a rickety old stool and it tipped a bit as Tara sat down, the light from a neon beer sign above glowing blue on her blond hair.

The bartender, a gnarled old man who wore his long gray hair in a single braid down his back, leaned toward them. He didn't speak but waited for their order. When Jake stepped around Tara, the old man's eyes widened in recognition.

"How do, Jake?"

"I've been better," he said. "How about you, Al?"

"Chief Barker has been making a real nuisance of himself," he said. "He's scaring off my regulars."

"Sorry to hear that," Jake said.

"Yeah, well, I just hope he nails that little rich bi—"

"Don't!" Nate cut him off.

Al glared as if he would throw Nate out for being so disrespectful, but Jake cut in.

"She didn't do it," he said. He put an arm around Tara's shoulders. "In fact, she's here with me and we're trying to figure out what happened that night."

Al turned his head and studied Tara. It was hard to tell what he was thinking. His dark eyes darted around her face as if trying to see into her soul.

"I didn't do it," she said. Her voice was soft and sincere, and topped with the big puppy eyes she was giving him, it was virtually impossible for him not to believe her.

Al seemed to make up his mind with a nod. "All right, but if you're lying, I hope you fry. Now, what can I do for you?"

"Do you remember me from that night?" Tara asked. "Did you see me talk to anyone or do anything strange?"

"Sorry," he said. "I was off that night."

His voice was genuinely regretful, and Brenna wondered if he was sad that he couldn't help them or because he was burdened with wondering if everything would have turned out differently if he had been here that night.

They ordered a pitcher of beer and Tara resumed trying to remember what happened.

"It *was* a different bartender," she said. "I remember now. It was a woman, large with a deep voice."

"That'd be Della," Al said. "She's off tonight."

"I remember, because I ordered an appletini from her and she laughed at me and called it a froufrou drink for silly girls," Tara said, looking peeved.

"That's sounds like Della," Al confirmed.

"So what did you drink?" Jake asked, looking amused at the frown on Tara's face.

"I believe she gave me a beer in a can," she said. "Pabst, she called it." Both men burst out laughing, and Tara looked sheepish and said, "It wasn't terrible."

Brenna glanced down the bar. A pale woman with dyed black hair cut in blunt bangs and a halter top over short-shorts and cowboy boots was watching them with a know-ing stare.

Brenna stepped away from the group, planning to ap-proach the woman, when her cell phone rang. She checked the number. It was the Bayview area; it had to be Dom.

"Excuse me," she said and stepped away from the noisy bar to take the call outside.

"Hello."

"Hi, gorgeous," Dom said. His voice was warm as if he knew she had just blushed. "How are you?"

"Doing well, and you?" she asked. The bouncer was watching her through half-closed eyes, very creepy, so she moved down the side of the building. She could see Tara and the others through the grimy window. They all seemed oblivious of the dark-haired woman sitting at the bar, still watching then.

"Right now I am hoping I earn enough brownie points to get you to go to dinner with me again," he said.

"Really?" she asked. He had her full attention now. "What do you know?"

"First agree to dinner," he haggled.

"I accept," she said. "Now spill it."

"Okay, okay, here's what I got from the floor manager at the paper mill. Apparently, the week before he died, Clue spent a lot of time talking about a new Harley Fat Boy he was going to buy."

Dom was silent and Brenna waited, but he said no more.

"That's it?" she asked. "You bartered dinner for that? That's not even worth a Hot Pocket on the T into Boston."

"Such impatience," he teased her. "I had to check my notes. Okay, a few days before he died, there was an incident in the break room at the mill, where one of the men, who lost his girl to Clue last year incidentally, called him out about the new Harley. There was a bit of a scuffle when the other guy said Clue was a liar, that he couldn't afford that sort of machine, but Clue said he had taken on an odd job that would pay him enough to buy it outright. When pressed, he refused to divulge what the job was, but there was a lot of speculation."

"Interesting," Brenna said. "Do you think Clue got mixed up in something illegal?"

"I wouldn't be surprised," Dom said. "He wasn't exactly squeaky-clean."

"But this gives us a whole other avenue of suspects," Brenna said. She was thrilled. "Dom, you're wonderful."

"I try," he said. "I'm going to keep poking around the mill and see if I can get more information."

"Thanks."

"So, what are you doing on this fine evening?" he asked.

"I'm with Tara at the Brass Rail, it's a dive bar on the edge of Morse Point. We're trying to jog her memory about that fateful night."

"I don't think I like the idea of you ladies being alone at a place like that," he said. "Why don't I come and meet you?"

Brenna glanced back through the window and saw Nate watching her. She gave him a small finger wave. He waved back. She did not want to have Dom and Nate meet up again if she could avoid it. There was just too much testosterone in the room when they were both present.

"Where are you?" she asked. She scanned the parking lot as if expecting him to pull up.

"Bayview," he said.

"Oh, we'll be long gone by the time you get here," she said. "Besides we're not alone, Jake is with us."

She did not feel the need to mention everyone who was in attendance. Again, she didn't want an overabundance of testosterone to complicate matters.

"Jake, the fiancé?" he asked.

"Yep, he has a vested interest in this," she said.

"I'll say," Dom said. "I hope it works out for him."

"Me, too. Thanks for calling me, Dom," she said.

"My pleasure. I'll keep you posted," he promised.

"Do," she said.

They said good night and Brenna shut her phone. So, Clue was expecting a big payout, but for what and from whom? She wondered if Chief Barker knew this, and I decided he must. He'd been out to the mill and to the bar; someone must have mentioned that Clue was bragging about money. Maybe that's why Tara hadn't been arrested. Maybe the chief knew more than he was letting on and Tara would soon be free of suspicion.

Then again, why did Clue end up in Tara's bed? Was it just bad luck on Tara's part to need a ride home on a night when Clue's enemy made a move on him? Or was it more personal? Was it someone like Maya Hopper, who wanted Jake back, and so used an opportunity to get rid of his best friend and have the blame dumped on his fiancée, clearing the path for her to win him back? It seemed unlikely, but anything was possible. In fact, Julie Harper still looked like a good suspect as the enraged stalking and pregnant ex, who finds the father of her unborn child in bed with another woman.

Brenna put her phone away and hurried toward the door, eager to share her news with Tara. When she arrived at the bar, the woman with the severe black bangs had worked her way to their group. Tenley and Matt had left the dance floor and were standing with the others.

"You're her, aren't you?" the woman asked Tara.

"I'm sorry?" Tara said.

"The woman they found in bed with Clue," the woman said, as if Tara was even dumber than she had supposed.

Brenna moved in beside Tara and looked at the Xena the warrior princess wannabe.

"What if she is?" she asked. "What's it to you?"

The woman leaned back and studied Brenna.

"Nothing." She shrugged.

"You're Valerie Scott," Jake said. "I worked on your Harley."

The woman turned her head toward him and gave him a once-over. It was an appraisal that was sexual in nature, but then, Brenna was pretty sure everything this woman did was like that, very elemental.

"You do nice work," she purred. "But you have terrible taste in friends."

Tara moved closer to Jake as if she could shield him from Valerie.

"What do you mean?" he asked.

"Clue Parker was your friend, wasn't he?" Valerie asked.

"Yeah, he was." Jake's voice was low, as if weighed down by the feeling of loss.

"I saw him drop it in her drink," Valerie said. She cocked her right hip, leaned against the bar, and crossed one cowboy boot over the other.

"Drop what?" Brenna asked.

Valerie rubbed her temples with her index fingers. "Gee, I am having such a hard time remembering now."

Nate stepped forward and slapped a fifty on the bar. "Memory coming back?"

"It's a miracle," Valerie said with a small smile. She

tossed her hair over her shoulder. "I can't say for sure, but I'd be willing to bet it was GHB, or you might know it by its street name—Bedtime Scoop."

"He drugged me?" Tara asked, looking wild-eyed.

"Now you're catching on," Valerie said. "I was sitting right over there and I saw you talk to some other blonde in red while he ordered a new drink for you, a cranberry and vodka, I believe. While you were chatting with the girlfriend, I saw him slip something into the drink."

"And you didn't say anything?" Tara asked.

"I'm saying something now," Valerie said as she tucked Nate's money into her bra. She turned to Jake, and said, "You may want to be choosier about your friends in the future. Clue Parker was a bad boy."

"Don't tell me you dated him, too," Jake said.

"I don't play on his team," she said. She winked and tossed her black hair over her shoulder. She sauntered away, leaving them all staring after her.

"Wow," Matt said. Tenley popped him with an elbow to the middle. He grunted and hugged her close.

"That's okay," she said grudgingly. "I think 'wow' covers it pretty well."

"How do we know she's telling the truth?" Jake asked. "She could have just been making all of that up because she recognized Tara from the newspaper."

"She's not," Tara said. "Clue did buy me a cranberry and vodka, because I wasn't drinking the Pabst. It's the last thing I remember."

Chapter 16

The six of them left the bar. No one spoke until they were outside.

"I don't understand any of this," Jake said. He began to pace back and forth. The bouncer frowned, as he was blocking the foot traffic in and out of the bar. Jake raised a hand in understanding and moved to the corner of the dirt lot. "Why would Clue do this? Why?"

"Actually, I think I may know," Brenna said. They all turned to look at her. They were standing in an oblong circle. She noticed that Tara moved closer to Jake and he to her as if to bolster each other from more bad news.

"Please help me to understand," Jake said. He looked desperate.

"That call I just got was my friend Dom Cappicola," she said. "He owns the paper mill where Clue worked. I asked him to let me know if he found out anything of interest about Clue."

"And?" Tenley prodded her.

"Well, it could be coincidence," Brenna said. "But Clue was bragging quite a bit about buying a new Harley."

Jake frowned. "He never said anything to me about that, and I always check his machines out for him. Plus, a new Harley costs fifteen thousand, easy, and there is no way he had that kind of money."

"He told everyone he'd taken on an odd job to pay for it," Brenna said.

"I can't believe that. He never said anything to me and I'm his best friend," Jake argued. "None of this makes sense."

"Unless the odd job was Tara," Brenna said.

Silence pulsed among the group as they collectively processed this information.

"You mean someone paid him to drug me and make it look as if we'd slept together?" Tara asked. "But that's sick. Who would do something like that?"

There was another beat of silence and Jake said, "Someone who doesn't want us to get married."

"But who—" Tara began, but Jake interrupted. "Your parents."

"No!" Tara protested. "I don't believe it."

Tenley stepped forward. "Tara, your parents are a lot like my parents; they have very high expectations for you. Don't you think it's possible?"

"No," she said. "It isn't."

"Oh, come on, Tara!" Jake threw his hands up in the air. "Your parents have been against this wedding from day one. Of course it's them."

Tara looked at him. Perfectly calm and serene, she held out her hands to him. Grudgingly, he took them.

"There is one thing I know," she said. "My parents would never do anything that would put me in harm's way. Ever. Do you really think they would pay someone to drug me and crawl into bed with me, especially someone like Clue, knowing how dangerous he could be?"

Jake took a deep breath through his nose and let it out. His shoulders dropped, and he looked at her and nodded.

"You're right," he said. "But if not them, then who?"

"There is the possibility that Clue wasn't being paid to ruin the wedding," Nate said. He rubbed his chin with the back of his hand and his gray eyes met Brenna's. "I never met him, but he seems the type who might always have a sort of get-rich-quick scheme happening."

"That was him," Jake conceded.

"Then do you suppose his odd job was actually his own plan to set up Tara by drugging her and making it look as if they'd gone to bed together so he could then blackmail her, say, to the tune of a new Harley Fat Boy?"

"I don't want to believe it," Jake said. "But from everything I'm hearing I don't see how I can't."

"It's just a possibility," Nate said.

"A good possibility," Brenna added.

He smiled at her, and Brenna was warmed from the inside out. Nate Williams was just too handsome for her own good.

"So, you didn't, uh, spend the night with him?" Jake asked.

"No, I tried to tell you that the detectives gave me a full examination, if you know what I mean?" Tara asked and Jake gave her a quick nod. "And there was no evidence of any, uh, action down there."

Both Matt and Nate snapped their heads away from the scene before them as if not wanting to hear any of it.

Tenley exchanged a glance with Brenna, who rolled her eyes. *Men!*

"Really?" Jake asked. The relief in his voice was palpable. He spun to look at the group. "Brenna, would you mind if Tara rides back into town with me?"

"No, not at all," she said. "I'll take everyone else in my car so you two can talk. Why don't I pick her up at the garage? It might not be a good idea for you two to be seen together."

"Why not?" Tara asked.

"Because we still don't know who the murderer is or why they went after Clue," Brenna said.

"She's right," Nate agreed. "Until we know what set the killer off, we should all maintain a low profile."

"I'll pull around in back of the garage," Jake said. "Meet us there."

"Will do," Brenna agreed.

Tara beamed at her, and Brenna hoped the conversation went well for her, for them both.

"Well, thanks for another memorable evening," Matt said, once they reached town. "One thing is certain, it's never dull with you two girls around."

"I miss dull," Nate said dryly.

Matt laughed.

"I need to pick up Tara at the garage," she said to Matt and Tenley, who were sharing the backseat. "Do you want me to drop you off at the shop?"

"Thanks," Tenley said. She glanced at Brenna's reflection in the rearview mirror. A look of understanding passed between them. Brenna was dropping them off to give Tenley time alone with Matt. And if Brenna was forced to be alone with Nate, well, these things happened.

She pulled into a spot in front of Vintage Papers. Tenley and Matt climbed out, and Brenna lowered her window to let in the sweet night air and, well, to eavesdrop.

"Can I walk you to your car?" Matt asked as they stepped onto the curb.

"Thank you," Tenley said. "I'm in back of the shop. Good night, Brenna, Nate."

"The ants go marching two by two," Brenna chanted and Nate finished with "Hurrah, hurrah."

She laughed, and he said, "I'll come with you to the garage. It's a little late for a woman to be out alone."

"Jake will be there," she said.

"True," he said. "But I'm coming anyway."

"Suit yourself," Brenna said, hoping she sounded more nonchalant than she felt.

They parked in front of Haywood Auto, which was closed for the night. The two bay doors were shut, so Brenna and Nate walked around the side of the building to use the smaller walk-in door. It opened when Brenna turned the knob and pulled.

"Hello?" she called. "Jake? Tara?"

A light was on in the back and Brenna made to go toward it, but Nate caught her by the elbow and held her back.

"I'll go first," he said. "It's dark. You don't want to skewer yourself on some equipment you can't see."

They picked their way around hanging hoses and tool carts until they reached the office.

Nate rapped on the door and Jake quickly opened it and ushered them into the small room.

"Sorry," he said. "We were waiting out front but Tara got spooked."

"It's been such a strange night," she said. She was sitting in a chair beside the desk. "I want to thank you, Brenna; if it hadn't been for you and Nate, that girl at the bar never would have told me what happened."

"I still can't believe Clue did that to you," Jake said.

"Do you suppose it was revenge?" Brenna asked.

"What?" Jake turned to look at her.

"I went to see Mrs. Sutton, Jake," she said. "I thought maybe she'd know something about Clue from Lisa. She told me that you and Lisa were planning to leave Morse Point together."

"We were," Jake admitted. "Until she left without me."

Tara took his hand in hers and entwined her fingers with his. She was trying to comfort him, which told Brenna that Jake had already told Tara all about Lisa, which was a good thing.

"Do you think Clue drugged Tara to make it look as if they'd spent the night together to get back at you for taking Lisa from him?"

Jake ran his free hand through his hair. "It's possible, but Lisa had broken up with Clue by the time she and I started seeing each other. Clue said he was okay with it."

"Did you believe him?"

"I wanted to," Jake said. His glance was rueful.

"Have you had any contact with Lisa since she left?" Nate asked. "Could she have come back and found out you were with Tara and gotten Clue to help her break you two up?"

"Nah," Jake shook his head. "Lisa is a free spirit. She'd never hurt anyone to get what she wanted." He let go of Tara's hand and opened a locker in the corner.

On the top shelf, he pulled out a small cardboard jewelry box. When he opened it, Brenna gasped. It was the angel she'd seen in the picture on Mrs. Sutton's hutch.

"She left me this in an envelope with my name on it," he said. "No note, no other explanation, she was just gone."

"Free spirit, indeed," Nate said.

Jake looked at Tara. "I think maybe it's time I give this to Lisa's mom. She can get it back to Lisa."

"That sounds good," Brenna said and noticed Tara's smile got brighter. "If you two want to say good night, I'll wait for you outside, Tara."

Brenna and Nate stood outside, looking at the town now in the midst of its nightly slumber. Crickets chirped, a warm breeze gusted across the town green, and the glow of the old-fashioned street lanterns that lined the side-walks lent the illusion of safety to the quiet community.

But it wasn't safe. There was a murderer out there, and Morse Point wouldn't be safe until Clue's killer was caught. A shiver caught Brenna by the back of the neck and she shuddered.

Nate gave her a swift glance and then pulled her close so that her side was pressed against the length of his. Neither of them spoke.

When Tara joined them, looking delightedly flushed, they silently walked her back to the inn where she was staying with her parents. Nate then escorted Brenna back to the Jeep before going to retrieve his own car.

"Well, I guess I'll catch the game highlights on ESPN. The Yanks were playing the Phillies tonight," he said.

"Yeah, it's interleague play. They always do that in June. It goes against my baseball purist leanings. It's a travel day for the Sox," she said.

"Yeah, so I have nothing to laugh about," he said.

"And I've been spared your trash-talking. How nice," she said. "I guess I'll just go home and dig into the brownie pie I made last night while I watch to see how badly your boys got trounced."

"Brownie pie?" Nate asked. "The one you make with the crushed pecan crust?"

"With fudge sauce on top," she clarified. "Yep, that's the one."

"If I swear not to trash-talk the Sox for a whole day, will you share?"

"Make it a week," she said.

He looked stricken.

"I think I even have heavy whipped cream to go on it," she said.

"Three days," he said. "That's the best I can do."

"Five days and a maraschino cherry," she haggled.

"Man, you fight dirty," he said. "Four days. That's my final offer."

Brenna took his outstretched hand and pumped it three times. "I'll bring the fixings to your place. Your TV is bigger."

Nate opened her door for her and Brenna climbed into the Jeep. He shut the door, and she rolled down the window.

"Hank will be thrilled to see you," he said.

"And me him," she agreed.

"Hey, is that why you're coming over, to see Hank?" He sounded a teeny bit miffed.

"Among other things," she said. She smiled and turned the key. Nate stepped back and she drove away with a wave. It felt good to keep him guessing.

Brenna stayed late at Nate's. They talked a little baseball and Hank got plenty of love, but mostly, they talked about Clue Parker and debated who his murderer could be.

Two slices of brownie pie each and still they had no answers. Brenna had the nagging feeling she was missing something, or overlooking something, but what? It was maddening.

"One more coat of polyurethane and this trunk will be ready for Betty Cartwright," Brenna said. She ran her hand over the recently dried varnish, checking its smoothness.

"We have to take pictures for the Web site," Tenley said. "This is one of your finest pieces."

"One of *our* finest pieces," Brenna corrected her. "We did it together."

They admired their handiwork for a moment. It was a quiet morning in the shop. Mrs. Delsum had picked up the birth announcements for her first grandson, and Mrs. Carter had ordered her daughter's engagement announcements. Other than that, the traffic had been minimal.

With a crash of bells, the front door was flung open and in came Ella and Marie Porter. They were trying to elbow each other out of the way as they charged into the shop.

"Did you hear?"

"Can you believe it?"

"Who would have thought?"

"His best friend!"

Tenley put up her hands to slow them down, but it was like trying to slow the running of the bulls in Pamplona. Brenna wasn't sure if she should hop up on the nearest table or look for a red cape to make them charge by her.

"What are you talking about?" Tenley asked as the two women stopped by the table.

"Oh, my, that really is lovely," Marie said, distracted by the hope chest on the table.

"Goodness knows, Betty Cartwright needs all the hope she can get," Ella said.

"Well, she is trying to wrangle old Saul Hanratty into a relationship," Marie said. "Personally, I'd hold out for someone with a little less nose hair."

"It matches her whiskers," Ella said.

"She doesn't—does she?" Marie asked with wide eyes.

"I saw Ruby tweeze them myself," Ella said. "Three big ones on her chin."

Marie's hand went self-consciously to her own chin.

"Ladies," Brenna said in exasperation. "What brought you charging in here? Surely, it wasn't to tell us that Betty Cartwright has a whisker issue."

"Jake Haywood was arrested," they said in unison.

"What?" Tenley cried.

"This morning," Ella continued. "Chief Barker showed up at the garage with a search warrant."

"We don't know the details, but he found a pair of bloody boots. They think it might be Clue's blood on them," Marie said.

"Oh, my God," Tenley said. She looked at Brenna in horror.

"Where's Tara?" Brenna asked.

"She's at the inn with her parents," Ella said. "Apparently, that's where they found Jake this morning."

"Do you think . . ." Tenley let the question dangle.

"No," Brenna said. She had no idea why, but she felt it deep down in her gut. "Jake didn't do it."

Tenley seemed to sag with relief.

"I'm going to go and see Tara," Brenna said. She hurried into the break room to grab her purse.

"I'll come with you," Tenley offered.

"You can't," Brenna said. "The Stuarts are coming in to discuss their wedding invitations."

"Darn it, come straight back here and tell me everything," Tenley said. "And tell her I'm thinking about her."

"I will," Brenna promised. She headed for the front door and felt Marie and Ella hot on her heels. She spun around and stared them down. "No. You are *not* coming."

They gave her looks remarkably similar to Hank's when he wanted something he shouldn't have. It didn't work for them either.

"Help Tenley with the shop," she said. "I'll be back as soon as I can."

The elderly twins gave her put-upon looks but headed to the break room to store their purses with only a smidgen of grumbling, just loud enough so Brenna could hear it but not really make it out. She gave Tenley an exasperated look and raced out the door.

It was a cool day for June, so Brenna decided to walk. The Morse Point Inn sat on a lush sweep of property on the south side of the town green. An imposing old Victorian, once the home of Elias Morse, Tenley's great-great great-great-grandfather, it was sold during the Depression to keep the family afloat. Since then it had changed hands repeatedly until it was bought in the 1970s and converted into an inn.

A tall black iron fence encircled the property and Brenna walked through the main gate and up the gravel walkway, lined with white azalea bushes, to the broad front porch. The house was white with black shutters and sported two turrets, one on each side, and a sloped mansard roof in the middle. Gingerbread woodwork decorated the eaves and gave the house an artistic flare. Brenna crossed to the red double doors. She pushed the one on the right open, and tapped the small silver bell on the wooden front counter.

Preston Kelly poked his head out of the office door behind the counter and looked relieved to see it was her.

"Brenna," he said. "I'm so glad it's you. I've been running interference for the Montgomerys all morning and it's just exhausting."

Preston Kelly was a tall, thin man in his early sixties. He was bald on top and kept the remaining hair on his head cut very short. He and his life partner Gary Carlisle had bought the inn a decade before and were the driving force behind the Morse Point Board of Tourism.

Brenna liked them, not only because they had bought several of her decoupage pieces for the inn, but because they shared her love of the arts and Morse Point was better for having them reside here.

"The press?" she asked.

"Yes," he said. "I actually had to turn the garden hose on Ed Johnson to make him get off my property. The man is a terrier."

Brenna laughed. She would have liked to have seen the local editor in chief get a good dousing. She'd had her own issues with him storming her front door a few months before.

"Is Tara here?" she asked.

"Yeah, she's upstairs in her parents' suite."

"Would it be all right if I went up?" she asked.

"Sure, I know you're friends, and Lord knows she needs one right now," he said. "It's the last door on the right."

"Thanks, Preston." Brenna dashed up the curved staircase.

She was halfway down the hallway when she heard the raised voices.

"Enough is enough, Tara," Mr. Montgomery was saying. "It is time for you to give up this romance and come home to Boston where you belong."

"I'm not giving up Jake." Tara's voice was high, tinged with tears and a little hysteria. "He didn't do it. I know he didn't."

"Then who did?" Tiffany's voice was lower than the others. She was obviously trying to keep it calm, but her voice was discouraged as if she couldn't believe Jake had let them down so terribly.

"I don't know, but it wasn't him," Tara said.

Brenna knocked on the door. It seemed as good a time as any to interrupt. She could tell they had all gone still on the other side of the door, probably expecting an onslaught from a reporter who had gotten by Preston.

"Tara!" she called. "It's me, Brenna."

The door was yanked open, and Tara hugged her close.

"Thank goodness you're here," she said against her shoulder.

"It's going to be all right." Brenna patted her back, hoping her words would prove true.

Tara stepped back. Her long pale hair was in disarray and her face was red and blotchy and streaked with tears. She was barefoot and wearing a pair of jeans and a lavender V-neck T-shirt. It looked as if she barely had the wherewithal to dress herself.

Brenna glanced at her parents. Tiffany and Tyler were in their usual neatly pressed and tidy attire. The only thing that gave away their distress was the strain etched in their faces in the tiny lines around their eyes and mouths like stress fractures in concrete.

Brenna had never seen that kind of strain on her parents' faces during her own struggles, and for a moment she envied the complete and unconditional love Tara received from her parents. She was a lucky girl. But then, perhaps that was why Tara was such a nice person: knowing only kindness had taught her to be unfailingly kind.

"You heard the news?" Tiffany asked.

"Yes," she said.

"It's not true," Tara said. She stood with her feet apart and her hands on her hips in a fighter stance. "Jake would never harm anyone, no matter what they had done."

"I don't think he did it, either," Brenna said.

"Great, just great," Tyler said sarcastically. "The paper artist says he's innocent, so gee, he must be."

"Daddy." Tara's voice was reproving. "Brenna is my friend and she's been very good to me, please don't talk to her like that."

"It's all right," Brenna said.

"No, it isn't," Tara said. "You understand what I feel for Jake. Mother and Daddy need to understand, too. This isn't a schoolgirl crush. It isn't a phase that I'll outgrow. I'm not going to come to my senses and leave Jake in a year or two. He is my soul mate, and I love him. My God, I love him so much sometimes I feel like I can't breathe without him. He is my heart, my life, my everything. If he goes to jail, I will live for the days that I get to see him. This is a love that will never die. Never."

As she spoke, Tara was transformed from silly, young

girl to strong woman. It was amazing. Brenna believed her—she would love Jake until the day she died—and judging by the teary expressions on her parents' faces, they did, too.

Tyler had the grace to look abashed and he cupped the back of his neck with his hand as he gave Brenna a sideways glance.

"My daughter is right," he said. "Please forgive my rudeness."

"Done," Brenna said. "I can't imagine how stressful this must be for you. Tara, did you tell them what we found out last night?"

"I did," she said. "I told Chief Barker, too, but he was so focused on taking Jake in, I don't know that he was listening."

"Don't worry," Brenna said. "I'm sure Jake will tell him, too."

"I hope so," Tara fretted. "I tried to go visit, but they won't let me see him."

"Does he have an attorney?"

"I have our family attorney representing him right now," Tyler said. "They are calling in their best criminal litigator."

"I just can't believe this is happening," Tara said. "I'd rather they arrested me. I want to go sit with the Haywoods, but I'm afraid they'll blame me."

"They have no reason to blame you for anything, sweetie," Tiffany said. She wrapped an arm around her daughter's shoulders. "None of this is your fault."

"If Jake hadn't started dating me, none of this—" Tara broke off with a sob, but Brenna interrupted her, "You don't know that. We don't know who killed Clue or why, and until we do, we can't go assigning blame. The only truly guilty party is the killer."

Tara gave her a weepy nod.

Brenna's cell phone chimed in her purse.

"Excuse me," she said as she fished it out of her bag. She didn't recognize the number.

"Hello."

"Brenna Miller?" a low voice asked.

"Yes," she said.

"It's Chief Barker. Could you come to the station at your earliest convenience, say, in fifteen minutes?"

"Um, sure," she said. "I'll be right there."

"Good," he said. He hung up before she had a chance to ask him what this was about, but judging by his tone it wasn't good.

Chapter 17

"I have to go," she said to Tara. "How about I talk to the Haywoods? I'll let them know how you feel and find out if there is any news about Jake."

"Will you?"

"Absolutely," Brenna said. "You eat something and get cleaned up and I'll call as soon as I can."

"Oh, thank you, Brenna." Tara gave her a bone crusher of a hug.

Brenna left the suite, trying to suck in enough air to get her lungs to reinflate.

She used her cell phone to give Tenley an update and then headed over to the jail. She could see several news vans parked out front and Ed Johnson holding court amidst a swarm of journalists.

She decided it might be better to enter stage right. She circled the building and used the back entrance, the one the police used, to enter the building.

She kept her head high and tried to appear as if she

knew where she was going. She knew from living in Boston that the people who stuck out were the ones who gawked or looked obviously lost.

The small station was abuzz. Phones were ringing, voices were loud, and everyone appeared to be in motion. Except for two people, who were sitting on a bench outside the chief's glass windowed office, John and Margie Haywood.

John was wearing his navy blue coveralls from the garage with his name embroidered over the left breast pocket in cursive. The knees were worn and the hems a little frayed, bespeaking the fact that John earned his living with manual labor.

Margie must have been at work at the elementary school already, as she was wearing a long, denim skirt with a medical scrubs shirt that had tiny kittens playing with balls of yarn all over it. She had on white tennis shoes and clutched her purse in her lap, much like a doctor would carry his black bag. Brenna would have laid odds that her purse was full of tissues, hand sanitizer, and lollipops.

Both of the Haywoods looked to be in shock. John was silently staring at the opposite wall, while Margie gently tapped her fingers on top of her bag, as if marking the seconds as they passed.

"Hi, Margie, John," Brenna greeted them as she approached.

"Oh, hello, Brenna," Margie said. "John, you remember Brenna Miller, she works over at the paper store."

"Jeep, 2003, had some brake work done a few months back," he said. "How're they holding up?"

"Fine, just fine," Brenna said. "Jake did a great job on them."

"He's a good mechanic," John said. His eyes skimmed past Brenna's to go back to staring at the wall.

"He is good," Brenna agreed. "And not just as a mechanic, but he's a good person as well."

Margie's eyes watered up and she patted Brenna's hand. "Thank you."

"I just saw Tara," Brenna said. Neither John nor Margie said anything, so she continued, "She'd like to come and be with you, and wait for Jake, but she doesn't want to intrude."

John and Margie exchanged a look.

"I don't know if that's a good idea with the press and all," John said. He glanced quickly at his wife as if deferring to her, and she nodded in agreement.

"I don't want her here," Margie said. Her lips, usually parted in a warm smile, were thin with anger.

Brenna's eyes widened. She wasn't sure what she had expected but it wasn't this tightly controlled rage.

"Maybe it's harsh of me," Margie continued, "but I do blame her. Jake was never in any trouble before she came around. Even when Clue tried to talk him into something foolish, Jake said no. He's a good boy, and now he's being arrested for a crime he didn't commit and it's all because of her."

"Now, Margie," John cut in, his voice soothing, but she snapped, "No! I'm not going to change my mind. He's better off without her. In fact, he's better off in jail if it keeps him away from her. She's trouble and I knew it the minute I laid my eyes upon her."

John watched helplessly while Margie fished a tissue out of her bag to dab her eyes.

"I'm sorry, I didn't mean to upset you," Brenna said.

Margie sniffed and dabbed her eyes again. Her voice wavered when she said, "No, I'm sorry, dear. I had no reason to take that tone with you. I just wish Jake had never gotten tangled up in this mess."

"That's understandable," Brenna said. She was relieved

to see a glimpse of the old Margie shine through her grief. Brenna couldn't imagine how awful it must be to have a son arrested for a crime he didn't commit. She supposed she'd have a hard time not blaming everyone around him as well.

The door to the office swung open and Chief Barker stepped out. His gray eyebrows went up a couple of notches when he took in Brenna.

"Can we see him?" Margie asked. Her voice was high-pitched and hopeful.

"I'm sorry, Margie," he said. "Not just yet. He's had some breakfast, however, so don't you worry about him."

"You let him know we're here, though, didn't you?" John asked.

"He knows," Chief Barker said. "Brenna, nice of you to stop by. Could you step into my office?"

"Sure." She gave the Haywoods a nod and walked through the door.

The chief's office looked much the same as it had upon her last visit. A large stuffed trout was mounted on one wall, several photos of the chief holding a string of bass were on another, and beside those were several pictures of the chief with his wife, children, and grandchildren.

If pictures told the whole story, Brenna judged the chief led a very good life.

She took the seat across from his desk. The padding was thin but it had armrests, she put her purse on the floor by her feet and waited for him to speak.

"So, I hear you were out with Jake and Tara last night," he began.

"Yes, that's right," Brenna said. "Chief, is this an official questioning?"

"Do you want it to be?" he asked.

"Meaning?"

"I can arrest you and ask you questions to make it more

official, or you can just answer me now as a witness, your call."

"Witness works," Brenna said.

"Tell me what happened last night," he said. "Don't leave anything out."

Brenna repeated the events of the evening. She figured Jake had already told him everything they had learned from Valerie Scott and that she was corroborating his story. She knew the chief would be checking with Tenley, Matt, and Nate as well so she tried to keep her account as accurate as possible.

The chief took notes while they spoke. When she mentioned her phone call with Dom Cappicola, he paused to study her face.

"I know the rumors about the Cappicola family," she said. "But Dom is different. He's trying to make the family business legitimate."

Chief Barker gave her a doubtful look and scribbled something in his notebook. Brenna wanted to peek, but she had a feeling it would say something unflattering about her intelligence quotient for befriending a mobster.

When she wound down by telling how she and Nate walked Tara home, the chief sat back in his chair and crossed his arms over his chest.

"So, what do you not understand about the phrase 'butt out'?" he asked.

"Are you going to yell at me?" she asked.

"I should," he said. "But I doubt it would do any good."

"Probably not," she agreed. She didn't like raised voices and was happy to discourage him from yelling.

"I am going to have to warn you, however, if you put one foot near this case again, I will arrest you for obstruction of justice or tampering with evidence, and if I can't make those stick, I'll nail you for jaywalking and make sure you stay locked up until the case is closed, am I clear?"

"Crystal," Brenna said.

"Now go," he said. "I have work to do."

"Yes, sir," Brenna said as she paused before opening the door. "Chief, one thing; did you know Julie Harper is pregnant with Clue's baby?"

He gave her a dark look and she said, "I found out by accident, I swear."

He started to stand and she quickly opened the door and stepped through it. "I'll see myself out, thanks. Bye."

She shut the door.

The Haywoods were no longer sitting on the bench, and Brenna wondered if they'd finally been allowed to visit their son. How awful. She could only hope that the chief moved quickly on what they'd found out and that Jake got out of jail sooner rather than later.

She went out the back door, checking to see that the coast was clear before she stepped outside. She wound her way around the two squad cars that were parked in the small lot and down the narrow alley until she was three buildings away from the station.

The town green was quiet today. Two mothers were sharing a blanket on the grass while their chubby-legged toddlers tried to catch the butterflies that fluttered overhead. An older couple sitting on a bench shared a newspaper and drank their coffee from paper take-out cups from Stan's.

Suddenly, Brenna had a craving for one of Stan's lattes in the worst way. Still, she had left Tenley alone longer than she'd expected. She had better get back to the store before Ella and Marie made her completely crazy.

Maybe she could convince Tenley to take a break by going to get them two of Stan's frothy masterpieces. The bells on the door handle jangled as she stepped into the shop. She had her sales pitch half figured out when she realized Tenley wasn't alone.

In fact, it seemed as if half of the town was in the small shop. The Porter sisters were still in attendance, as well as Sarah Buttercomb, Lillian Page, Matt Collins, and Bart Thompson, to name a few.

"I thought I'd throw a little party," Tenley said in answer to Brenna's questioning look.

"So, I'm fashionably late?" Brenna asked.

"Indeed," Tenley said.

"Seriously, what's going on?" Brenna whispered.

"Ella and Marie started dragging people in off the street to talk about Jake's arrest," she said. "It's not looking good for him."

"He must have done it." Ruby from the salon was addressing the group. "I mean, can you imagine finding your bride in bed with your best friend? It would drive even the nicest man to commit murder."

"No, no, no," Lillian Page argued. She had a cup of Stan's in one hand and a cream puff from Sarah's bakery in the other. "Jake is a good man. He'd never hurt his friend, no matter what he'd done. I can't imagine how his parents are suffering right now."

Brenna could have told her, but she wanted to hear what the others had to say. She made her way toward the worktable, where there was a pile of cream puffs and a twelve-pack of Stan's coffees. Ah, life was worth living again.

"I'll bet Brenna can tell us more," Ella Porter announced.

Nuts! Only the Porter twins could wilt an inch of froth in one breath.

"I really don't know anything," Brenna said.

"Aw, come on, Brenna," Bart Thompson said. "You're the one who figured out who murdered Mayor Ripley last April; you must have some idea of who killed Clue."

"Actually, I thought his wife murdered him," she said.

"I only figured out who really killed him by almost getting killed myself."

"Really?" Bart looked disappointed.

Brenna noticed the rest of the room looked glum, too. Oh for Pete's sake, they didn't really think she had it all figured out, did they?

"Well, I guess I'll just get back to my shop," Ruby said. "I left Katie Barker under the dryer. She's going to frizz."

Was it Brenna's imagination or was Ruby giving her a once-over that found her wanting? *Hmm.* More people made excuses, and sure enough the shop was cleared out in a matter of minutes.

"Well, how very efficient of you," Tenley said as she stared in bemusement at her now empty shop.

"I did shower today, I swear," Brenna said, and Tenley burst out laughing.

"They just want you to tell them who did it," she said. "How rude of you not to know the answer."

"That's me," she said. "The rude Bostonian."

"It's okay, I love you anyway," Tenley said. "So, the chief called me."

"He wants you to come in," Brenna guessed.

"Yes," she said. "Do you mind watching the shop while I go?"

"Not at all," Brenna said.

"Is he very mad at us?" Tenley asked.

"Mostly me, I think," Brenna said. "Given my track record and all."

"I'll check in as soon as I'm out," Tenley said. With a wave, she left, and Brenna sat down at the table to contemplate the rest of the cream puffs and the question of who murdered Clue Parker.

Nothing of any significance came to Brenna that afternoon. She helped Carole Fenton with her music box. She had attended Brenna's decoupage class months before and had decided to try a music box of her own. It came out well, but her varnish had bubbled so Brenna showed her how to use superfine sandpaper to buff it down and reapply so it wouldn't bubble.

She was just beginning to wonder where Tenley was—surely, she couldn't still be talking to the chief—when the front door banged open and in strode Jake Haywood.

"Jake? You've been released?" she asked.

In his wake danced a beaming Tara, followed by her parents, his parents, and Tenley.

"The judge granted me bail," he said. "And Mr. and Mrs. Montgomery posted it."

"Really?" Brenna asked. "That's fantastic!"

"Given my ties to the community, I'm not considered a flight risk," Jake said. "Although, I'm sure it helped that Mr. Montgomery has golfed with the judge several times in the past few weeks."

"I never thought I'd say this," John Haywood said, "but I think I may have to take up the game."

He and Tyler shared a strained laugh while the wives gave tight smiles. Jake took Tara's hand in his as if she were his lifeline and he wasn't about to let go.

"Jake, what about the boots?" Brenna asked. "I heard they found them in the garage."

He shrugged and shook his head. "I can't figure it out. They're an old pair that I never wear because they're too small. They've been kicking around the garage forever."

"Did you ever loan them to anyone?" she asked.

"No," he said. "Actually, I thought I'd gotten rid of them a while ago."

"Where did they find them?" Brenna asked.

"Shouldn't we leave this to the police, dear?" Margie asked. "I'm sure Chief Barker will figure it out. He's a good man."

Brenna nodded at the gentle rebuke. Margie was right. Jake had just been released; he didn't need her grilling him like a drill sergeant.

"I'm sorry, you're right," she said. "Jake, I'm just delighted that you're out and I want it to stay that way."

"Thanks, Brenna," he said. "I do, too."

"In any case, it was pretty flimsy evidence based on the crime scene investigator's report that there was a bloody boot print in the carpet of Tara's bungalow. They went looking for a pair of boots, but anyone could have planted those," Tyler Montgomery said. "I'm sure that's why they gave you a reasonable bail."

"If you call a million dollars reasonable," Tiffany said with a sniff.

"I am sorry, ma'am," Jake said. "I'll make it up to you, I'll pay back every penny, I swear."

"And I'll help," John Haywood vowed. "I can never thank you enough for getting my son out of there."

"Don't you worry about it," Mr. Montgomery said. "We take care of our own. We have a ways to go until you're a free man, but my attorney says they don't have much in the way of evidence against you. He thinks this case will be, and I quote, 'a slam dunk.'"

"Oh, Daddy," Tara sighed, and threw her arms about her father in a big hug. She looked over his shoulder at Brenna and said, "We're all going to the Fife and Drum for a celebratory dinner. Do you two want to come?"

"Oh, that sounds lovely," Tenley said. Her face turned pink when she added, "But I have plans."

"Me, too," Brenna said, not wanting to be the fifth, or in this case, the seventh wheel.

"Another time then?" Tiffany asked.

"Definitely," Tara and Brenna said together.

They watched the group leave, and Brenna turned to Tenley and said, "You have plans?"

"A movie date," she confirmed. "With Matt."

"Whoa," Brenna said. "When did that happen?"

"While we were sitting in the hall waiting to talk to Chief Barker," she said. "He asked me out and I said yes."

Brenna hugged her friend. "I am so happy for you."

"Thanks," Tenley said. Then she looked at her wristwatch. "Oh, my, is that the time? I have to go. I told Ruby I'd be stopping in for a quick overhaul. Do you mind closing the shop?"

Brenna laughed at the panic in Tenley's eyes. It was ridiculous because Tenley could show up in a Hefty bag and galoshes and still be a knockout. That's what flawless skin, capped with long blond hair and big blue eyes, could do for a gal. Honestly, if she didn't love Tenley like a sister, she'd probably want to back over her with her car.

Tenley left with a wave and Brenna locked the door behind her. What a day! All she wanted to do was go home, pour a glass of wine, and put the murder of Clue Parker out of her mind for a night.

It was difficult, of course. Whenever she thought of the murder, she couldn't help but wonder who had perpetrated such a vicious crime. The Montgomerys were an obvious pick, but as Tara said they would never put her in danger—besides they were each other's alibi.

Tara was the next logical choice given that she'd been found in bed with the body and holding the murder weapon, but all the evidence seemed to point to her having been drugged, and Brenna still had a hard time wrapping her mind around Tara being cold-blooded enough to murder someone. Jake was a likely candidate, especially with the boots as evidence, but Brenna couldn't believe it. Jake wasn't the murdering kind either. Yes, that was a subjective opinion, but there it was. Besides, the one thing Brenna couldn't let go of was if Jake had stabbed Clue in a passionate rage then why didn't he stab Tara as well? Of course, Clue had plenty of exes who wanted him dead, and maybe it was one of them, but none of the ones she'd met so far seemed to have murder in mind. And yet, someone had murdered Clue. There had to be something she was missing.

Then again, with Jake released on bail, maybe it would all be okay. Maybe the chief would discover who the real murderer was and Jake and Tara could have their happy ever after. The thought made Brenna smile.

She cleaned up the shop, putting away supplies and sweeping the floor to gather up all of the stray paper clippings. She emptied the coffeepot, washed it, and put it in the dish rack to dry overnight.

She flipped the sign on the front door to Closed, and turned out the lights. She exited out the back door, which opened into the alley. It was late and the alley was unlit. She had parked her Jeep behind the shop today as the spots in front had all been full.

She had not anticipated closing alone. Perhaps it was an urban flashback, but a whisper of caution skidded over her skin. Brenna paused. She had left through the alley loads of times over the past two years, but tonight it felt different. Maybe it was because she usually left with Tenley, or maybe her Spidey sense was just in overdrive; either way she couldn't shake the tingling feeling that something was very wrong.

Her years living in Boston had taught her to be cautious, especially alone at night in an alley and she laced her keys through her fingers and kept her pepper spray ready. She walked with her back to the wall, giving herself optimum visibility, the Jeep was just a few feet away now.

A hiss and a screech sounded and Brenna jumped, her feet actually leaving the ground, as a blur of fur sped past her and then another, brushed against her jeans and stomped on her toe. *Cats!*

She sagged against the wall. Obviously, knowing there was a murderer out there was getting to her. She pushed off the wall and hurried to the Jeep.

She was just a few feet away when she heard the crunch of steps behind her. She spun with her keys ready to gouge when she was smacked on the back of her knees, knocking her legs out from under her. Before she could brace herself, she hit the pavement, cracking the side of her head on the concrete. A starburst of pain exploded behind her eyes.

"Brenna! Brenna!" The shouts sounded far away, too far to help her. She heard a dog bark. She could hear footsteps running, one going away and one coming closer. She couldn't tell which one was moving faster.

"Brenna, can you hear me?" It was a man's voice.

She forced her eyes open, but the large shape looming above her was inscrutable in the dark. Still, she'd know that voice anywhere. It was accompanied by a canine whimper as a big shaggy blond head loomed over her.

"Nate, Hank," she said. She wanted to tell them to chase her attacker, but her voice failed her as everything went black.

"How is she?" a voice whispered. It was a kind voice, and it sounded familiar. Brenna wanted to reply but found she was too groggy.

"She's suffered a head trauma, but the scan looks good, no signs of fracture or bleeding. She'll be all right," said another woman's voice, which she didn't recognize. "Right now, she just needs plenty of rest."

This sounded like a fine plan to Brenna and she let herself be lulled back into sweet oblivion.

She could feel sunlight shining on her face, beckoning

her to wake up and face the day. Brenna turned away from it and her head throbbed.

She winced and reached up to press her brain back into her skull, because surely pain like this could only be caused by her brain trying to make an escape, and felt a wad of gauze where her temple used to be.

"What?" She pried her eyes open and discovered she was in a hospital room, mauve and gray, very soothing and somewhat familiar, with a curtain drawn around her bed for privacy.

Tenley was curled up in a contortionist's position in a green vinyl chair in the corner. She was snoring softly. Brenna realized it was her voice she had heard the night before. She felt her chest squeeze tight with affection for her friend.

"Hey," a low voice said to her right. *Nate.*

She turned and then cringed as a union of hammers pounded on the inside of her skull in response to the sudden movement.

"Sorry," he said. He leaned on the bed rail to examine her more closely. "How are you feeling?"

"A half step above roadkill," she said. "What happened?"

"You were attacked," he said.

His voice was grave, and Brenna knew it was because he was aware of her past, that she operated at a certain level of paranoia at all times because of the robbery that had all but ruined her two years ago in Boston. He probably figured this was going to send her right around the bend.

Probably, a year ago it would have, but she was made of sterner stuff now. She thought about the night before and it came back in flashes; the alley, getting hit, the ambulance ride, the hospital. She even had a vague recollection of getting up in the middle of the night last night to use the bathroom, which was probably why her room seemed familiar.

No, this wasn't like Boston. She was in much better shape this time, and when she found out who did this to her, she was going to kick their—

"Hey, you're awake!" Tenley unfolded her leggy length from the chair and moved to the other side of the bed. She took Brenna's hand in hers. "How are you feeling?"

"Angry," Brenna said. "I don't suppose the person was caught?"

Nate took her other hand and squeezed it. "Sorry. Hank and I found you on our way back from getting ice cream at Stan's. You were unconscious. The only thought I had was to call 9-1-1 and get you to the hospital."

Brenna understood—she would have done the same— and yet, she was bitterly disappointed. This attack had to be because of the murder. Someone wanted her to stop asking questions and they were being very clear in getting their point across.

"You're awake, Ms. Miller." A woman in a white coat walked into the room. "I'm Dr. Gershon."

While she studied the chart clipped to the end of the bed, Brenna studied her. Dr. Gershon was short and stout, and on the younger side of forty with just a hint of wrinkles in the corners of her eyes and her hair professionally high-lighted. She wore severe-looking black-framed glasses, and Brenna couldn't help but wonder if they were really needed or if she wore them to make herself look smarter.

"Nice to meet you, Doctor," Brenna said.

"You've suffered a head trauma before," Dr. Gershon said.

Brenna felt both Nate and Tenley stiffen beside her.

"Yes, but it was on the other side," she said.

"Very good." The doctor seemed pleased that she knew

this one was different. "I'd like to look at your pupils, if that's all right."

"Sure," Brenna said. She moved her eyes the way Dr. Gershon told her to, avoiding direct eye contact with her penlight. She answered a few basic questions and the doctor seemed satisfied. A nurse was called in and together they unwrapped Brenna's head.

The doctor probed the wound, which smarted, but Dr. Gershon assured her it was just a nasty bruise and that her shoulder had taken the brunt of her contact with the ground. The backs of her knees were badly bruised and it hurt to move her legs, but Dr. Gershon told her nothing was broken. Then they rewrapped her head with enough gauze to stuff a pillow.

"Have you been up on your feet at all?" Dr. Gershon asked.

"The nurse took me on a walkabout earlier," Brenna said. "I had to use the bathroom."

"How'd that go?" Dr. Gershon asked.

"Fine," Brenna said. She wished the gauze covered her whole head as she could feel her face get hot as she discussed her bathroom success with Nate in the room.

"Your head took quite a blow," Dr. Gershon said. "There's no sign of bleeding or a fracture. You're very lucky. I'm going to okay your release, but I'll want to check you in a few days and you'll need to have a ride home. No driving for a couple of days."

"I can take her," Nate volunteered. "We're neighbors."

"I'll start getting your papers in order," Dr. Gershon said. "Call me immediately if you have any symptoms of severe headache, nausea, seizures, or difficulty with walking."

"Will do," Brenna said. "Thank you, Dr. Gershon."

The doctor smiled and left.

"Has Chief Barker been by?" she asked them. "I want to file a report."

"Early this morning," Nate said. "He said he'd stop by later."

An enormous bouquet of daffodils appeared in the doorway, followed by the Porter twins.

"My dear, it's all over town," Ella said as she moved into Nate's space, forcing him out while she plopped the overflowing vase on Brenna's rolling tray. "You were attacked!"

"And big, brave Nate came to your rescue," Marie said. She beamed up at him, and Nate was forced back even farther from the bed.

"Thank you for the flowers," Brenna said. "They're lovely."

"Well, you'll need them to cheer you up," Ella said. "We saw Chief Barker in the lobby and he's on his way. He doesn't look very happy."

"Who doesn't look happy?" Chief Barker asked from the door.

"Stan at the diner," Marie lied. "The froth on his latte was flat today."

Chief Barker lowered a bushy gray eyebrow at her, but she just blinked at him, the picture of innocence.

"Do you all mind if I talk to Brenna alone for a minute?"

It was posed as a question, but it was clearly an order. The four of them reluctantly left the room.

"Am I in trouble again?" she asked.

"What do you think?" he asked.

"Yes?"

"Do you want to file a report?" he asked. He unfolded a sheet of paper from the inside pocket of his jacket, and Brenna knew it wasn't negotiable.

The next twenty minutes were spent with Chief Barker asking her specific questions about the attack. Brenna was disheartened to realize that she didn't remember much of anything and hadn't even gotten a glimpse of her assailant. The chief looked pretty down about it, too.

"Why do you think you were attacked?" he asked.

"I don't know," she said. "It's not as if I know anything about the murder that you don't know, so why attack me?"

"Unless Clue's murderer thinks you know more, in which case, they're either trying to scare you or kill you, too."

"Comforting," Brenna said.

"I'm going to have Officer DeFalco monitor you while you recover. He'll maintain a schedule of drive-by check-ins until we catch who did this," he said. He glanced at the gauze wrapped around her head. "Nice hat, by the way."

"Is that supposed to be funny?" she asked.

"Just to me, apparently," he said.

"You think I had it coming," she accused.

The humor was wiped off his face like an eraser took chalk off a blackboard. "No, I'd never want to see you hurt. But that is a heck of turban you've got going."

Brenna frowned. "Mirror. Stat."

Chief Barker looked bewildered and patted his pockets as if he might have one handy. "Hey, I'm not a girl. I don't carry a compact."

"The bed is on wheels," she said. "Just scooch it so I can see the mirror in the bathroom. I was too fuzzy-headed to look before."

He did as he was told, and Brenna got her first glance of herself in full hospital headdress.

"My God, it's the size of a fruit basket," she said. "I look like I should have a pineapple and some grapes up there."

Chief Barker pressed his lips together beneath his mustache, obviously trying not to laugh, and patted her shoulder. "It's not that bad."

She glared.

"Okay, it is that bad, but you do carry it off with a certain flair."

"Don't you have murderer to catch?" she asked.

"Yes, ma'am." Chief Barker headed toward the door. She heard his bark of laughter as soon as the door shut.

Chapter 18

Nate refused to let her take the bandage off once they were in his truck, so he was on her bad list as well.

She bit back a moan of pain when she climbed out of the truck cab. The pain in the backs of her legs was severe and if she were any less stubborn, she might have cried. When she started across the grass to her cabin, Nate stopped her with a hand on her elbow.

"What do you think you're doing?" he asked.

"Going home," she said. She thought it spoke well of her that she didn't add "duh" to the end of her sentence.

A bark sounded and Hank came tearing across the lawn to greet her. Brenna reached down to pat his head, careful not to bend over too far and give herself a walloping headache.

"That's too far of a walk," Nate said. Before she could protest he scooped her up into his arms with only the smallest of grunts. He was careful to keep his arm up away from the bruises on the backs of her knees.

"You don't have to carry me. I think I can manage it," she lied.

"Yeah, and when you faint halfway there, who is going to look like the big jerk for letting you hoof it?" he asked.

"That would be you," she said.

"Precisely," he said. Hank trotted beside them as if appointing himself her backup carrier.

As Nate strode across the grass, Brenna marveled that after months of daydreaming about being in his arms, she finally was and, surprise, it wasn't anything like she had pictured it. *Go figure.*

Of course, she had pictured them sharing an embrace after a nice dinner date when she was having a particularly good hair day, not when her head was wrapped up like a stuffed cabbage and she had hospital antiseptic stink on her.

She did notice that she liked the smell of him, however— it was woodsy and masculine. And she liked that he hadn't actually broken a sweat while carrying her.

"Oh, my heavens, is that Brenna?" A shout came from a nearby cabin and Twyla came out with Paul and Portia Cherry, two of Nate's other renters, on her heels.

All three were somewhere in their fifties, retired from other careers, and enjoying life lakeside while pursuing their art.

"What happened?" Portia asked. She was a former nurse, who worked primarily in glass and was married to Paul, a retired economist, who worked in clay.

"Brenna had an accident," Nate said. He stepped up onto Brenna's porch and made for the door, but she stopped him, gesturing toward her cushioned wicker love seat instead.

The sun was warm and the breeze was cool. It was a perfect day in June, and she wanted to sit outside and soak up the beauty around her for a while. Although she hadn't allowed herself to dwell on it, she was very much aware that the attack last night was probably intended to be fatal.

"An accident?" Paul asked. "With what?"

"It's okay," Brenna said to Nate. "You can tell them."

"Brenna was attacked behind Vintage Papers last night," Nate told the others as they crowded up onto the porch.

"What?" Portia asked. "Is there a fracture? A hematoma? Shouldn't you be at the hospital?" Once a nurse, always a nurse.

"I was," Brenna said. "They did a CT scan, and I'm fine unless I suddenly lose my ability to walk or form sentences."

"Tea," Twyla said. "I'm going to brew you some of my peppermint tea. It's good for headaches. It'll fix you up in a jiffy."

Twyla hurried back across the lawn with a twirl of her raspberry skirt.

"Was it a burglar?" Paul asked. "Did you catch someone trying to break into the shop?"

"No," Brenna said. "They came up behind me when I was going to my car, and the next thing I knew I was down and Nate and Hank were there."

Paul's and Portia's heads swiveled in unison to Nate for his portion of the story.

"Hank and I had just run into Matt and Tenley on their way to a movie, and they said Brenna was still at the shop, so I figured I'd stop by so Hank could see her. He misses you."

Brenna smiled and scratched Hank's ears. He had stationed himself beside her like a sentry keeping watch.

"When I got there, she was on the pavement and her assailant was running. I think he must have heard us. Anyway, I stayed with her instead of giving chase."

"Good decision," Portia said. "There's no telling what would have happened if you hadn't found her."

They all sat with her while she drank the tea Twyla brought her, which amazingly did seem to help. The conversation moved away from Brenna's melon to other happenings around town, the upcoming women's auxiliary rummage sale, the Elks Lodge brass band's next concert, and the proposal to lower the speed limit on Route 9. As if by silent consent, no one spoke of Clue Parker's murder or of Brenna's attack.

When the tea was gone and the sun was higher in the sky, Brenna let out a big yawn. The others took this as a sign to let her get some rest. Twyla promised to bring her some soup, while Portia offered to re-bandage her head for her tomorrow.

"Come on," Nate said. "I'll help you up."

He helped her to her feet while Hank sat and watched, as if he knew she was frail and was afraid he might knock her down with his exuberance.

Brenna knew she should have welcomed the restful silence of her small cabin after the noise and bustle of the hospital. Instead, the quiet seemed ominous, as if whoever had done this to her was just biding their time, waiting to get her alone. Brenna shuddered. She hated feeling weak and afraid. It reminded her too much of those crippling days in Boston after the gallery had been robbed.

"Hank and I are going to stay and keep watch," Nate said when they reached her bedroom. He raised his hand as if expecting an argument. "This is non-negotiable."

Brenna would have argued, but she didn't have it in her. With a grateful smile, she went to spend some quality snuggle time with her pillow.

It was the sound of ice cubes rattling in a glass that awoke her first. It was followed by the sound of hushed voices, both male and female. Hmm.

Brenna sat up slowly, but was delighted to find her head no longer throbbed. She felt weak, probably from not eating all day, and was surprised to find it was dark in her room and outside. She had slept the day away.

She pushed back her covers and carefully put her feet on the floor. She hadn't forgotten Dr. Gershon's words about suddenly losing her ability to walk, and she didn't want to add a face plant on her hardwood floor to her list of injuries.

A bark sounded and she knew that Hank was still in residence, which she found very comforting. The door to her bedroom eased open and a familiar blond head appeared.

"Hi," Tenley said and gave her a sympathetic smile.

"Do I still look that bad?"

"Well, it's just . . ." She gestured to Brenna's head.

Brenna rose and looked in the mirror. Yep, the mammoth gauze chapeau was still on her head, only now it had shifted and loosened. She must have had a restless sleep, and it looked like she was wearing a lopsided beehive.

"Is Portia around?" she asked.

"Outside with everyone else," Tenley said.

"Everyone else?"

"Nate, Twyla, Paul, Matt, Tara, and Jake are here and Officer DeFalco keeps popping in," Tenley said. "Marie and Ella were here but the early bird special at Stan's started at four and it's meat loaf tonight."

"He makes a good loaf," Brenna said. She looked back at her reflection and sighed.

"I'll go get Portia," Tenley offered.

"Thanks," she said.

There was a sharp rap on the door and she turned to greet Portia. But instead of her sturdy neighbor with short gray hair and glasses, in strode tall and stocky with an energy force field all his own.

"Dom!" Brenna said. She fought the urge to dive under her covers.

"I'm going to kill him," he said. "Whoever did this to you, I am going to kill."

"I appreciate the sentiment, but given that you're trying to reform the family image, you should probably rein it in a little."

Dom cupped her chin and stared into her eyes. His dark brown gaze was magnetic and Brenna couldn't look away as his eyes swept over her as if reassuring himself that she was fine.

"Are you all right?" he asked.

"I called your house this afternoon and your landlord told me what happened," he said. "I'd have been here sooner, but I was down in Bayview and the rush hour traffic was thick."

"You didn't have to come. It's not as bad as it looks," she said. "Trust me."

"I want you to come back with me," he said.

"Pardon?" she asked. She surely hadn't heard him correctly.

"Bayview," he said. "I think you should come back with me. You could have some rest and relaxation by the beach, get away from the situation here, and basically stay out of harm's way."

"*Harm* being a murderer?" she asked.

"Yeah," he said. "I have to be honest, Brenna, I don't like this."

"You should try wearing the headdress," she said. "You'd like it even less."

"Nice to see you haven't lost your sense of humor," Dom said. He leaned forward and kissed the side of her forehead not covered in gauze.

Someone coughed. It was the fake sort of clearing of the throat that alerted you that you were about to be interrupted. They broke apart, Brenna with more haste than Dom.

She turned to find Nate standing in the doorway with Portia.

"Portia said she could change your bandage now, if you'd like," Nate said. His gaze moved to Dom, and he said, "Sorry to interrupt."

Brenna wondered if it was just her imagination, but he didn't sound one bit sorry. Portia moved past both men and came to stand in front of Brenna. She plopped a steel first aid kit on the bed beside her and popped the latches.

"It's okay," Dom said. Then he grinned. "We're just figuring out the logistics of Brenna's coming to Bayview with me. I think it would be best to get here out of here for a while."

Nate's gray eyes darted from Dom to Brenna. He studied her for a moment with his usual laser-like scrutiny. He watched Portia unwind the bandages from around Brenna's head, then he turned back to Dom and said, "I think that would be for the best."

With that, he left, and Brenna was stuck trying to decide which man she wanted to slap more.

It took her an hour to convince Dom that she wasn't going anywhere. He wasn't happy, but when Tenley offered to bunk with her for the night, which made Matt unhappy, there really wasn't much more anyone could say.

Brenna ate some of the potato chowder Twyla brought over, and after reassuring everyone that she was fine, she left it to Tenley to shoo them all away while she went back to bed.

She slept through until morning, and aside from the goose egg on the side of her head, covered by a much smaller bandage from Portia, she almost felt normal again.

Refusing to sit around her cabin like a useless lump,

Brenna insisted on going into work with Tenley, who didn't approve but was smart enough not to say so.

Halfway through the day, Brenna wondered if perhaps she should have stayed home. The bells on the door were an incessant jangle, to the point where she and Tenley stopped looking up when they rang.

Brenna had been afraid that in the aftermath of the attack, she would begin to twitch at the slightest movement around her. She desperately didn't want to become the timid mouse she had been after the burglary in Boston. She shouldn't have worried. It was virtually impossible to be nervous as she was never ever alone.

In fact, if one more person stopped by the shop to ask how she felt, she was going to take the cigar box she was working on as a demo for her class into the bathroom to finish it in solitude.

The Fife and Drum sold cigars in the bar, and Matt had been saving the wrapper labels for Brenna for months. He'd also donated several empty cigar boxes. Brenna had hoped to use them in her class tonight, but it wasn't going to go very well if she couldn't finish her project.

She had flattened the ring shaped wrappers in a flower press, making them easier to apply. Using white glue, she applied the labels around the edge of the box. It wasn't as finished as she would have liked, but her students were getting pretty savvy, so perhaps it was enough to give them a starting place.

"I'm partial to a good Havana myself," a voice spoke from behind her.

Brenna turned to find Nate smiling down at her.

"Hi," she said. "What brings you here? Don't tell me you're going to sign up for my class."

"I will if it's the only way to keep an eye on you," he said. He was smiling, but she got the feeling he was serious.

"I'm fine," she assured him. She patted her new bandage. "See? I've even been downsized to only slightly lumpy."

He glanced up and she followed his gaze and noticed the entire shop had gone still. The Porter sisters in particular were leaning close, trying to hear their conversation without being too obvious.

"How about some fresh air?" he asked.

"I'd like that," she said. "Let me just put away my project."

Nate waited by the door while Brenna put her box on a nearby shelf to dry. Tenley met her at the table and said, "You go. I'll finish up."

"Thanks," Brenna said. She ignored the whispers that followed her as Nate held the door for her and they made their escape.

"You never learn, do you?" she asked.

"What?"

"The gossips are going to go mental over this," she said.

"Does that bother you?" he asked.

"No," she said. "I'm getting used to it."

"Me, too," he said.

They walked in silence, and Brenna was pleased to discover that it was comfortable. Apparently, they didn't need to talk baseball to be at ease with each other.

The steady cadence of mallets pounding tent spikes filled the air. The town green was being set up for the Morse Point Women's Auxiliary rummage sale. Brenna was looking forward to the annual event. Last year she had scored a wooden bench that she had decorated with paper cutouts of tulips and then finished with a beaded fringe around the bottom edge. Lillian had bought it to put in the reading nook in the library, and Brenna always felt a lift when she saw someone sitting on her bench. She hoped to find something like that tomorrow. With Betty Cartwright's hope chest done, she needed a new project to challenge her imagination.

As she and Nate sat on a vacant park bench, she spotted Jake and John Haywood setting up the booths on the green with several other men, including Tyler Montgomery. Brenna waved at them and all three waved back.

"How are you feeling?" Nate asked. "And tell me the truth. I don't want any of that brave soldier stuff."

"I'm much better," she said. "It doesn't hurt as much when I walk. I've had no headaches or blurry vision. The bump only hurts when I touch it, so of course I have to keep poking it, so I can tell myself, yup, still hurts."

He grinned, and Brenna suspected he'd done the same thing with his own boo-boos in the past.

"So, I was wondering . . ." His voice trailed off, and Brenna said, "Yes?"

"Why didn't you go to Bayview with Dom?"

He looked uncomfortable, as if he didn't want to ask, but he couldn't stand not knowing even more. Brenna knew exactly how he felt.

"I'm not running away from my life here," she said. "It's a good life and I'm happy."

"It's dangerous for you to be here," he said. "Dom can't be happy about that."

Brenna shrugged. She supposed she could tell him that she and Dom were just friends, but she wasn't sure if that's what he was asking, and she didn't want to make an idiot of herself by assuming. Besides, she really wasn't sure what the future held for her and Dom. He certainly seemed willing to wait for her to figure it out, and maybe when she did, it would be him that she chose.

She wasn't one to let an opportunity pass by, however, so she turned to him and said, "I've got one for you now."

"Okay," he said.

"Why did you go to Connecticut?"

His eyebrows rose and he turned to study her. A small smile played on his lips as if he was pleased by her question.

"It was my mother's birthday," he said. "She lives on the shore in Noank so my brother and I went for the weekend."

No girlfriend! No romantic tryst with another woman! Brenna resisted the urge to jump up and down, knowing it would hurt her head and she'd embarrass herself, but inside she was tap dancing.

"What are you smiling about?" he asked her.

"It's a lovely day, isn't it?" she asked.

"It is," he agreed.

Nate treated her to a latte to-go and brought her back to Vintage Papers. Ella and Marie were pressed against the front glass, waiting for her. They scrambled away as soon as she opened the door and she turned and smiled at Nate.

"Told you so," she said.

"Maybe we should give them something to talk about," he said and winked at her.

Brenna felt her mouth slide open in surprise but anything she might have said was interrupted by Tara, who came banging out of the open door and grabbed her in a bear hug that about crushed her.

"Oh, Brenna, you're here. I've been so worried," she said.

"There's no need. I'm tougher than I look."

She glanced over Tara's head at Nate. What had he meant by that wink? Oh, if only Tara had been a couple of seconds slower. *Nuts!*

He smiled at her and waved good-bye. Brenna waved back, feeling acutely frustrated to see him go, but knowing she couldn't exactly call him back.

"The class is waiting for you," Tara said. "Sarah brought scones and Tenley made tea. You should get off your feet."

Brenna let Tara lead her into the shop. Her class was assembled and ready to go. She noticed the surreptitious glances they gave her as if checking to see if she was about to faint.

It felt good to have the concern of so many people. Although she'd only lived in Morse Point for two years, it was beginning to feel more like home than any other place she'd ever lived. Brenna felt lucky to be so accepted by these people and this community.

She spent the class working with each of her students individually. She helped Sarah get her labels laid out just right, and she listened to Lillian's latest stories about her boys. She navigated a dispute between the Porter sisters over how much glue to use, and finally, she checked on Margie Haywood, who had spent half of the class at the window, overseeing the setup of the booths for tomorrow.

Unfortunately, Margie's cigar box looked like a beginner's. The labels had too much glue and they were uneven.

"Are you okay, Margie?" Brenna asked.

"Yeah, sure," Margie said with a brave smile. "I just haven't been sleeping what with all that's been happening and the women's auxiliary to top it off. Maybe I should try this again when I can give it my undivided attention."

"I have a million of those sorts of pieces," Brenna said. "I used to be stubborn and try to force it, but I've found it's better to walk away and come back to a piece that's being difficult. Sort of like doing a crossword puzzle. If you put it down and pick it back up later all of a sudden, the answers just come."

"Thank you, dear," Margie said and patted her hand. "You're being very kind. Now enough about silly old me, how are you feeling?"

"Better every day," Brenna said. "Especially, because I feel certain that it is just a matter of time before Clue's killer is caught."

"I'm sure you're right, dear," Margie said, but she looked at her with grave concern, making Brenna think she didn't really believe Clue's killer would ever be caught. But perhaps as the mother of the chief suspect, she just couldn't let herself believe it until it happened and her son was safe.

"Are you making yours for your future husband?" Ella Porter asked Tara.

"Yes." Tara beamed with pleasure.

She had done a wonderful job of trimming her labels into sharp edged stars and putting them together so that they resembled a star patterned quilt. Brenna was impressed with her eye for color and detail.

The bells on the door handle jangled, and Jake walked in. He surveyed the room until he found Tara and then he crooked a finger at her. She flew across the room and into his arms. A collective sigh was emitted from the women gathered, including Brenna.

Jake took Tara by the hand and approached his mother.

"Dad says it's okay with him, but we have to ask my mom," he said to Tara as they circled the table.

Margie looked up at their approach and gave them a small smile.

"I thought you were helping your dad," she said.

"I was, but I need to ask you something," Jake said.

"I'm all ears," Margie said. She glanced around the room as all motion had stopped. "Shall we go outside?"

"No, I know you're going to approve," he said. He was grinning from ear to ear like he'd just won the lottery.

Maybe he had. Maybe the chief had found the real murderer. Brenna leaned closer. She was getting as bad as the Porter sisters.

"Mom, Tara and I are getting married," he said.

"I know, dear," Margie said. She looked at him as if he were being silly.

"No, I mean we're getting married tomorrow," he said.

Margie's eyes went wide and her mouth popped open, but no sound came out.

"I know it seems sudden, but we know what we want. We're going to have a small ceremony at city hall, and we're putting a down payment on a small house over on First Street."

"Jake, this is so sudden," Margie said. "I mean, there's still a murder investigation going on and we don't know what's going to happen . . ."

Jake waited until she wound down, then he looped his arm about Tara's shoulders and pulled her close.

"I know that either of us could be tried for Clue's murder," he said. "We both know that, but we talked about it and we know we're innocent. We think that getting married and buying a house is the strongest act of optimism that we can make to show that we believe in us, for now and forever."

Tara beamed at Jake, and he leaned down and kissed her. A collective swoon swept through the room, and Brenna saw Tenley surreptitiously wipe the corner of her eye.

Margie's hand fluttered around her throat as if she didn't know what to say. When Jake and Tara parted and turned to look at her, she raised her hands in helpless surrender and pulled them both close for a hug.

"Well, congratulations are in order I expect," she said.

"Thanks, Mom," Jake said. "Now since we won't be having a big wedding, I asked Dad if we could have the money you set aside for our wedding for the house, and he said it was fine by him but I should ask you."

"Oh, well, let's discuss it outside," Margie said.

Her eyes were wide and she glanced at the other ladies in the room. Brenna knew she must be wondering what everyone thought of this sudden turn of events. To reassure her, Brenna gave her a big grin before she turned to the refreshment table in order to give the family some privacy.

The Porter sisters were almost falling out of their chairs in their efforts to hear what was happening, so Brenna took them both by the elbows and asked, "Scone? Tea? How about it ladies?"

Ella sent her a withering glance and Marie sighed as if still enthralled with Jake's speech.

Brenna had just taken a teacup off of the tray when she heard Tara whisper to Tenley, "Since my parents posted his bail, Jake refuses to ask them for any help with the house. He has such integrity. Luckily, the owners of the bungalow are looking to get out, so we're getting quite a steal. The Realtor said fifteen thousand would be an excellent down payment. I am so excited."

"You should be," Tenley said. "It's really wonderful news."

Brenna watched the door shut after Margie and Jake. A dull thud in her chest made her peer out the window after them. Margie was standing on the sidewalk, wearing her usual khaki skirt and scrubs top.

Today, however, she was wearing loafers instead of those old boots of Jake's she'd been stomping around in. The ones she had said she was going to donate to the rummage sale, the ones Brenna had teased her about getting hot pink laces for, the same ones that had been worn to commit a murder.

She watched Margie enfold Jake in a hug, fierce, almost as if she were saying good-bye. A roaring noise filled her ears and as it grew louder, Brenna clutched the edge of the refreshment cart and put her teacup down with shaky fingers. Fifteen thousand dollars was a lot of money, the kind of money that could buy a Harley Fat Boy outright.

She didn't pause to consider her actions, she just felt herself move across the floor.

"Brenna!" Tenley called after her, but she ignored her. She had a killer to catch.

Chapter 19

Margie had left Jake, who had gone back to help his father, and was headed across the green toward the bank.

"Margie, wait!" Brenna called.

Margie glanced over her shoulder. Her eyes met Brenna's, but instead of slowing down, she broke into a run.

Her knees screamed in protest, but Brenna didn't slow down. She dashed across the street after Margie. There was a screech of brakes and a car honked at her but Brenna kept going. She left the cement walkway and cut across the grass, vaulting over bundles of tarps still to be set up for tomorrow's event.

Jake and John Haywood glanced up from the booth they were erecting and stared as first Margie and then Brenna ran by them.

"Margie, stop!" Brenna yelled. She was gaining on her, and managed to grab her arm and spin her around. They were both wheezing from the spontaneous sprint and

Brenna's head was pounding as the blood rushed into her bruised temple.

"It was you," Brenna said. She was gasping for breath but she didn't let go of Margie's elbow. The older woman tried to wriggle out of her grasp, but Brenna held firm.

"You can't prove anything," Margie protested as she bent over to catch her breath.

"The money," Brenna said. "The amount Jake asked you for is the same amount Clue expected to be paid for doing an 'odd job.' Was the odd job to drug his best friend's fiancée and make it look as if they'd slept together?"

"No!" Margie protested. "It wasn't supposed to happen like that."

Margie's eyes opened wide at her own admission of guilt. The Haywood men were crossing the green toward them, and Margie started to panic. Brenna tightened her hold.

"What happened, Margie?" Brenna asked. "How did it all go wrong?"

Margie sagged as if the fight was seeping out of her.

"He was supposed to seduce her, not drug her. I was there to take photos and convince Jake that she had cheated on him. But Clue demanded more money and I didn't have it," she said. "He threatened to tell Jake what I'd done. I couldn't let him. You have to understand."

"So, you killed him," Brenna said. She felt queasy, and not just from the pounding in her head. This woman she had liked so well was a murderer, and none of them had seen it.

"I had no choice," Margie said.

"Why did you come after me?" Brenna asked. Margie looked at her with sad eyes. "Oh, the shoes. You were afraid I'd remember that you wore Jake's old boots and put it all together."

"I didn't want to hurt you," Margie said. "I like you."

Brenna felt a bone-deep chill inside.

"Why, Margie, why did you do this?"

"Because *she* was going to take away my baby," Margie said. Jake and John were almost upon them. "She would have taken him to Boston or someplace even farther away and I might never see him again. I couldn't let her have him."

"Oh, my God," Brenna said. A blast of intuition hit her right between the eyes. "Lisa Sutton is dead, isn't she? You killed her."

Margie's head snapped up and she looked at Brenna with a crazy light in her eye. "She tried to lure him away. She was a wicked girl. I did what I had to do."

"Mom, what's going on?" Jake asked as he joined them.

"Nothing, dear, I'm just having a chat with Brenna." She looked softly at her son and laid her free hand on his cheek. She gazed at him with love, and then she stepped back and yanked her elbow out of Brenna's grasp. She spun on her heel and bolted for the road.

"Margie, watch out!" John Haywood shouted and pointed at the road.

"Mom!" Jake Haywood yelled as he looked in the direction his father pointed and saw a large dairy truck headed their way.

"Oh no you don't!" Brenna shouted. She bolted after Margie, knowing exactly what she planned to do. Brenna wasn't about to let her get off that easy.

She sprinted across the grass, leapt over a hedge, and made a dive, catching Margie around the knees and bringing her down into the dirt. This time it was Margie who smacked her head on the ground as she cushioned Brenna's fall.

A pair of shiny, black boots stepped into her line of sight. Brenna glanced up to see Chief Barker looking down at her and thoughtfully pulling on his mustache.

The dairy truck rolled by, and Margie dissolved into sobs. "Why didn't you let me do it?"

"Because it's not fair to Clue or Lisa," Brenna said. She gingerly climbed off of Margie. "Chief Barker, you're going to want to take her in for the murders of Clue Parker and Lisa Sutton."

The chief leaned down and pulled Margie up by the arm. John and Jake ran up to meet them, and Brenna stood on wobbly feet. Her head pounded and she was out of breath, but it was worth it.

"Don't hate me," Margie said to her husband and son.

"What's going on?" Jake glanced from Brenna to Margie and back.

"Please take me away, Chief," Margie said. "I'd rather not be seen like this."

John glanced at his wife and his eyes grew sad. "Oh, no, Margie, not you."

She didn't look at him but brushed at the dirt that smeared her skirt. She refused to speak or look at anyone.

"Brenna, you'll follow?" Chief Barker asked, although it didn't sound like a question.

"I'll be right there," she agreed. "Just let me catch my breath."

He gave a nod and led Margie across the street to the station house.

"I don't understand," Jake said. "What's going on?"

Tara came running across the green to join them with Tenley on her heels.

"It was your mother," John Haywood said. "She murdered Clue."

"What? That's crazy!" Jake protested.

"And Lisa Sutton," Brenna said.

Jake staggered back and sank onto a bench. Tara knelt beside him as if she could shield him from the bad news.

"I don't understand," Jake said.

"Your mother has always been afraid of losing you," John said. "That's why she became the school nurse, so she could be near you every day. I thought she was just being overly protective."

"B-but . . ." Jake stammered as if he couldn't comprehend what was happening.

"Damn it! I knew something was wrong," John said. "She hasn't been herself. Ever since Jake and Tara started up, I'd catch her pacing around the house, up at all hours, frequently muttering to herself. I knew something was bothering her, but I never thought she'd . . . oh, poor Clue."

"And Lisa," Brenna added.

John looked sick to his stomach and sat down next to Jake.

"Lisa?" Jake asked. "She killed her?"

"I'm afraid so," Brenna said.

"Then Lisa didn't leave me her angel, did she?" Jake asked. He looked devastated.

"No, I think your mom did that to ease your pain," Brenna said.

The group was silent. Brenna met Tenley's gaze, and saw the devastation there. This was Margie Haywood, bandager of boo-boos and giver of hugs.

"So why did she kill Clue?" Jake asked.

"He was supposed to seduce Tara away from you, and your mom planned to take pictures to prove it, but instead he drugged her," Brenna said. "He threatened to tell you what Margie asked him to do if she didn't give him more money. She panicked."

"Oh, God." Jake buried his face in his hands, and Tara held him tight.

"I'm sorry, Mr. Haywood," Brenna said.

John Haywood looked at the bandage on her temple and shook his head. "No, I'm sorry. She could have killed you, too. You did what had to be done."

John broke down, and Jake slid across the bench and wrapped his arms about his father. Tenley put an arm around Tara and held her while the two men sobbed.

"I'd better go," Brenna whispered. "Chief Barker is expecting me."

"I've got it covered here," Tenley said. "We'll follow in a bit."

This time Brenna glanced in both directions before crossing the street to the station, but really, she couldn't imagine feeling much more run-over than she did at the moment.

Two weeks later, Tara and Jake were married in a quiet ceremony at city hall. A small reception at the Fife and Drum followed, with his father and her parents in attendance as well as the Porter sisters, Matt, Tenley, Nate, Dom, and Brenna.

Margie Haywood had confessed to the murders of Clue Parker and Lisa Sutton. Jake had given Lisa's pendant back to her mother and the family had decided to move away from Morse Point and the painful memories that surrounded them here.

Clue had no family, his parents having passed away years before, but Jake made sure he had a nice funeral and was buried in Morse Point Cemetery. A headstone with his favorite motorcycle engraved upon it had been ordered with the epitaph "Whatever it is, it's better in the wind."

After a filling steak dinner, Tara and Jake cut into a delicate whip cream cake with strawberry filling and served it to all of their guests.

A small pile of wedding gifts had been placed on a table

by the door, and Brenna was surprised when the hope chest she had just delivered to Betty Cartwright appeared on the table with a big blue bow and a note that read: *"We think you two young people can make better use of this than us. Be happy. Best wishes, Mr. and Mrs. Saul Hanratty."*

"So, Betty got her man?" Tenley asked.

"It seems so," Brenna said.

"May I have this dance?" Matt appeared at Tenley's elbow and held out his hand.

Jake and Tara and the Montgomerys were already waltzing on the small dance floor by the large fireplace in the corner. Brenna watched as Matt led a beaming Tenley onto the floor.

She glanced at the large table in the corner. John Haywood was seated with the Porter sisters on either side of him, each doing their best to get his attention and keep him from dwelling on the fact that his wife was not here to share this momentous occasion in their son's life. John was attentive to the two ladies, but every now and then, just for a second, Brenna saw him glance at his son and look happy and proud, but with a tinge of sadness.

"Care to dance?" Dom asked. Brenna turned to find him standing beside her. In another impeccable suit, he was mouthwateringly handsome, and she wished, not for the first time, that her feelings were not already tangled up around her landlord.

She glanced back at the table. Nate was in conversation with John while the Porter sisters appeared to be squabbling about something, probably John Henry and whether he had been in love with Ella or Marie.

"Sure," she said and put her hand in his.

Dom moved her carefully around the floor as if still cautious of the injuries done to her head and her knees. She was about to tell him she was fine, when she caught a movement over his shoulder.

It was Nate. He was leaving. As if aware of her eyes upon him, he paused at the door to raise his hand in good-bye. She lifted her fingers off of Dom's shoulder in return.

As the door shut, Brenna couldn't help feeling as if her heart had left the building with him. Then Dom pulled her close, and she let him. If she had learned one thing from Margie Haywood, it was to not hold on too tightly to what she wanted but rather to let it be.

Decoupage Projects

Decoupage Glass Votives

White glue or decoupage medium
Votive candleholder (clear glass)
Paintbrush
Paper cutouts (flowers, butterflies, etc.)
Tissue paper
Candles

First, apply a thin layer of glue on the votive and position your first paper cutout, which should be thin enough to let the candlelight through, on the glass. Brush over the cutout with more glue. Then press a wide strip of tissue paper (a pale color is best) over the paper cutout and brush on more glue. Work your way around the votive, making sure there are no air bubbles in the tissue paper, until it is completely covered in cutouts and tissue paper and a final coating of glue. Once it is completely dry, light a small votive candle inside of it and watch it glow.

Decoupage Block Puzzle

White glue or decoupage medium
Six two-inch blocks
Six four-by-six-inch pictures
Foam brush
Scissors

Place a block on the picture and use it to trace six even squares. Now cut the picture into six squares. Place the pictures on top of six blocks, re-creating the original picture, and glue each picture onto its corresponding block. Let them dry completely. Using the five remaining pictures, repeat the previous steps on the five remaining sides of the blocks. Now you have a six-sided puzzle. To make it last longer, you can use more glue or polyurethane to make a protective coating on each side of the blocks.

"Well, what do we have here?" Ella Porter asked. "Is that Nate Williams driving with a young woman I've never seen before?"

"It is," Marie Porter, Ella's twin, confirmed.

Brenna Miller reared up from her crouched position at the back of the Jeep and smacked her head on the open hatch door. Ouch!

She clapped a hand on her head and turned to follow the directions of the sisters' gazes. Sure enough, Nate's vintage pickup truck was leaving a trail of dust behind it as he roared up the drive toward the communal lot where Brenna was parked.

The trees that lined the road behind him were ripe with the vibrant autumn colors of candy apple red and golden butterscotch. The late September sun was warm but the air held a bite of the New England winter rapidly approaching.

The windows of the truck cab were down and Brenna saw Nate flash a smile at her as he pulled up beside them.

As always, she couldn't help but return his smile. The man was a charmer for sure.

He climbed out with a wave and circled around to open the door for his companion. The first thing Brenna noticed was that she was young. Her wavy brown hair was styled in a bob, reminiscent of a flapper from the twenties. Her jade green earrings dangled and she smiled up at Nate as he helped her out of the truck. She carried a vintage carpetbag and wore a cute yellow dress with a slightly poofy skirt that ended at her knees, very retro.

Nate walked over to Brenna and the Porter sisters with the young woman beside him.

"Good afternoon, Brenna, ladies," he said and he inclined his head.

The twins, who were within bragging rights of reaching their seventieth birthday, twittered beneath his attention, while Brenna said, "Hi, Nate."

"Let me introduce your new neighbor," he said. He gestured behind him. "This is Siobhan Dwyer. She'll be staying in the cabin next to yours for a while. Siobhan, this is Brenna Miller, one of our resident artists. I let Brenna stay here even though she likes the Red Sox, because she makes the best brownies in town."

The Porter sisters glanced between Nate and Brenna with identical looks of speculation. She could only imagine what the two gossips were thinking, that she and Nate were shacking up, so she'd best diffuse the situation before things became awkward.

A bark came to her rescue as Hank, Nate's golden retriever, came bounding up the hill as if he hadn't seen Nate in days instead of just hours. Jumping up on his hind legs, he licked Nate's face and then turned to jump on Brenna as well. While she rubbed his ears, Nate retrieved his tennis ball from the grass and threw it back down the hill toward the lake. Hank set out after it with a happy bark.

"You also put up with me because I'm a great dog sitter," Brenna said.

"Hank does adore you," Nate agreed with a smile that crinkled the corners of his eyes, and made Brenna hope he wasn't just talking about Hank.

"Well, I guess I know who to see when I want a brownie," Siobhan said, bringing the attention back to herself. "Although, I find too many sweets can ruin a girl's figure. But then, you're not exactly a girl, are you?"

Brenna blinked, uncertain of whether she'd just been insulted or not. She decided to write it off as a bad attempt at humor.

"No, I'm definitely a grown-up," she said with a forced chuckle. "Welcome to Morse Point, Siobhan."

She held out her hand. The young woman hesitated and then brushed Brenna's fingers with hers for just the briefest moment. Her fingers were icy cold and Brenna resisted the urge to rub her hands together to warm them up.

She turned and gestured to the elderly twins. "These ladies are Ella and Marie Porter. We've just gotten back from a furniture salvaging expedition over in Auburn and they're helping me unload."

Siobhan looked the women up and down but did not offer her hand. "A pleasure."

"Likewise," the sisters said together. They didn't sound very sincere.

"Nate, would you be a love?" Siobhan asked as she ran her hand down his arm and then motioned toward the back of the truck. There were several boxes, an easel, and what appeared to be a stack of canvases. "I'm just exhausted from my trip."

"No problem," he said.

Brenna and the Porters watched as he hefted a few of the boxes and headed down the trail toward the cabin. Siobhan followed behind him, carrying nothing, not even her carpetbag, which she'd left on the ground at their feet.

"I don't like her," Ella hissed when Siobhan was out of earshot.

"You don't like anyone," Marie said.

"So?" Ella asked. "That doesn't mean I'm wrong about this one. There's something very cat chomping on a canary about her. I'm only surprised feathers don't fly out of her mouth when she speaks."

"You're exaggerating," Marie said. "What do you think of her, Brenna?"

"Nate must have a reason to be renting to her," she said. Although, privately, she couldn't imagine what it was since, like Ella, she did not get a warm and fuzzy feeling from the girl.

"Oh, lookie here," Ella said from beside Nate's truck. "Someone certainly has a high opinion of herself."

She had peeled back the brown paper wrapping from one of the canvases and revealed a portrait that was obviously Siobhan. It was very Frida Kahlo, a headshot with a severe expression done in bold colors.

"Ella, get away from there," Brenna demanded.

She glanced at the cabin to see if Nate and Siobhan were returning.

Marie leaned in close and said, "The name in the corner is Siobhan. It must be a self-portrait."

Ella dropped the paper wrapping back over it and curled her lip in distaste. "A very high opinion of herself it seems."

"That's not for us to say," Brenna said. She turned back to the Jeep and pulled out a drawer from the dresser she had found in the secondhand shop and handed it to Marie.

"I wonder where she's from," Marie said as she cradled

the drawer and headed down the hill toward Brenna's cabin. "She's definitely not from around here."

"How can you tell?" Brenna asked, handing another drawer to Ella before taking the last one herself.

"We'd know her people," Ella said as if it were obvious.

"You don't know everyone," Brenna said.

"Yes, we do," they said together.

Brenna rolled her eyes. The twins were an information superhighway unto themselves, no doubt, but even they couldn't know everyone.

The three of them wrestled the bulky dresser out of the back of the Jeep. They were about to heft it down the hill when Nate came sprinting up to them.

"I'll get that," he said.

Ella and Marie sagged in relief and dropped their end on the ground.

"You don't have to," Brenna said.

Nate just gave her a penetrating stare as he lifted the small dresser out of her arms and made his way down the hill with it.

"So nice to have a man around." Marie sighed.

"Indeed," Ella agreed. "And just look at the way his back muscles bunch, why I bet he could pick me up with one hand."

Brenna and Marie gave her identical looks of disbelief.

"What?"

Brenna shook her head, refusing to comment. She helped the sisters pack their own treasures from the secondhand store into their Buick and waved as they headed down the dirt drive to the main road. They departed quickly as Marie was driving and she was well known for being heavy on the accelerator. Brenna cringed slightly when Marie didn't stop at the end of the drive but hauled that Buick carcass across two lanes and sped toward town.

Thankfully, there were no other drivers on the road at the moment.

She perched herself on the open back of her Jeep and played fetch with Hank. She told herself it was because he looked lonely, but she knew better. Her eyes kept straying toward her new neighbor's cabin, and she knew she was waiting for Nate to make an appearance. He had taken the last load of stuff to Siobhan's after he had helped her with her dresser. Not that it was any of her business who this girl was, or why she was here, still, she had no intention of moving until she saw Nate come out of her cabin.

Hank dropped a slobber covered ball at her feet and she scooped it up and threw it across the meadow that stretched out behind the row of cabins on the other side of the lake. Hank took off in a flurry of fur and Brenna glanced back to find Nate walking back up the hill toward her.

"You spoil him," he said as he sat on the open back of the Jeep. "I had a perfectly well-behaved dog before you came along."

Brenna scoffed. "Oh, please, I'm the disciplinarian. You're the pushover."

"Ha!" Nate said. "Who lets him eat at the table?"

"Beside the table not *at* it," she corrected. "Who lets him sleep in the bed with his head on the pillow?"

"He keeps me warm," he argued.

As if he knew he was the object of their conversation, Hank wagged his way over, nudging his head between them, demanding love.

They both obliged and when their hands collided in his fur, Brenna moved hers to run down his back, wondering if Nate felt the same spark of awareness she felt or if it was all in her head.

"So, a new tenant?" she asked.

"Temporarily," he said. "She's a friend of an old art

school buddy of mine. He e-mailed me last week and asked if she could stay here for a few weeks."

"Oh, so she's not from around here?" Brenna asked.

Nate grinned. "The Porter sisters could tell, eh?"

"Yeah," she confirmed.

"I figured," he said. "Honestly, I don't know much about her. I picked her up at the train depot in Milstead. She'll be here for a few weeks. She seems nice enough."

"Hmm." Brenna said nothing more.

"So, are you up for the game tonight?" His gray eyes met hers and as always, Brenna found it impossible to look away.

"I don't know why you put yourself through the torture," she said. "You know the Red Sox are going to spank your sad little Yankees right out of any hope they have to make the play-offs."

"Spoken like a truly deluded member of Red Sox Nation," he said. He rose and stretched his back. "Eight o'clock, my cabin, big screen, be there."

Brenna grinned. "I'll bring pie. Chocolate cream, okay?"

"Oh, yeah," he said. "For chocolate cream, I'll even let you boo my team once."

"Twice," she haggled.

"Once per slice," he countered.

"Deal," she said.

"Oh, and I invited Siobhan to join us," he said. "Since she's new in town and all, it seemed the neighborly thing to do."

Brenna frowned. Nate had never been concerned with being neighborly before.

"That's okay, isn't it?" he asked.

"Oh, yeah, it's great!" she said, forcing a smile. Big fat lie.

She watched him walk away with Hank at his side, knowing that the ridiculous jealousy she felt meant that the crush she'd had on him for the better part of two years had not diminished one little bit. Darn it. Like the common cold, someone really should have invented a cure for this condition by now.